KEEP STILL

G·K
Hall
&Co.

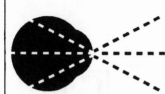

This Large Print Book carries the Seal of Approval of N.A.V.H.

KEEP STILL

ELEANOR TAYLOR BLAND

G.K. Hall & Co.
Thorndike, Maine

Published in 1996 by arrangement with
St. Martin's Press, Inc.

G.K. Hall Large Print Mystery Collection.

The text of this Large Print edition is unabridged.
Other aspects of the book may vary from the original edition.

Set in 16 pt. Bookman Old Style by Minnie B. Raven.

Printed in the United States on permanent paper.

Library of Congress Cataloging in Publication Data

Bland, Eleanor Taylor.
    Keep still / Eleanor Taylor Bland.
        p.   cm.
    ISBN 0-7838-1931-5 (lg. print : hc)
    1. MacAlister, Marti (Fictitious character) — Fiction.
    2. Afro-American police — Illinois — Fiction.
    3. Policewomen — Illinois — Fiction. 4. Large type books.
    I. Title.
[PS3552.L36534K44   1996b]
    813'.54—dc20   96-30509

To Barbara Richardson, Lake County Coroner, who handles a very difficult job with competence and compassion.

To Carolyn Murray, DCFS, who loves the little children and knows they are precious in His sight.

To Ted, who cares.

ACKNOWLEDGMENTS

A very special thank you to Brad Hettlinger for professionalism, competence, flexibility, and humor. Thanks also to the Red Herrings for support, encouragement, and excellent critiques, and to Carol Edwards for outstanding copyediting.

For technical assistance I would like to acknowledge Mark Agin; Larry and Scott Beatty; Jeff Caretta; Hameeda Carr, Children's Counselor, LACASA; Keith Corbin, Leo Delaney, and Elliott Dunn; Eunice Fisko; Refugio Garcia; Ann January Howell; Sharon A. Laughlin, Coordinator, Haines Museum, Waukegan Park District; Kathy Lay, ACSW, LCSW; Jerri Mercer; Raymond I. Olson, Waukegan Symphony Orchestra; Jerome Pietrzyk, Ph.D.; Ed Plese; S. Louise Powell; Bruce Rasmussen; Mary Robinson, North Chicago Public Library; and Esther Martinez.

PROLOGUE

It was after seven o'clock when Sophia Admunds remembered the laundry that had been in the washer since morning. She was on her front porch, watching as Neda, her neighbor across the street, stopped pinching back petunias long enough to straighten up and massage the small of her back. As Sophia sat in the big old slat-backed chair that she had rocked in as a child on her mother's porch, the evening songs of sparrows and mourning doves stilled and the crickets' songs began. The sun went down and the stars came out and the last of the june bugs flickered just above the snapdragons.

As Sophia watched, Neda collected her gardening tools and waved as she went inside. Half a dozen neighbor children bicycled by, calling, "See you later" and "Meet you at the basketball court." Then, with the younger children gathered inside and porch lights turned on, the street became quiet.

Sophia pulled a sweater around her shoulders, enjoying the cooler evening air, reluctant to get up. She had lived here for seven years now, in this small, cramped house that was nothing like the sprawling Victorian twelve blocks from here and half a world away where she had raised her children. That house was sold after Warren had his first stroke and the stairs and the distance from the bedroom to the bathroom became too much for him. Warren had been dead for six years. Now her children wanted her to leave this house, too, and move into an even smaller place, one of those senior citizen condos with a kitchenette, two rooms, a balcony, and quilting classes or some such in the recreation room.

She didn't want to move anymore. Neda was her age, seventy-one, and the neighbors on either side were in their fifties. Farther down the block, younger couples raised the children that filled the street with laughter and arguments all summer. She could sit here and pretend she was in her old house again, pretend that Warren was just inside, or remember both of them young. She was neither sick nor senile, and she lived frugally enough to make the pension, Social Security, and Warren's investment income last longer than Warren junior said they would. And if there wasn't quite enough, her children could help her.

She had stayed home and raised them. Warren had worked long hours to put all four of them through college and had given them the down payments on their homes as wedding gifts. Maybe, if she lived long enough, it would become their turn to take care of her. Sophia didn't see anything wrong with that.

The air grew cooler, and she thought of the laundry again, the load in the washer and the load on the floor waiting to go into the washer. She got up, noting the stiffness that seemed to be getting worse. She was not as young or as spry as she used to be, and she felt somewhat relieved at the thought of slowing down.

Inside, Sophia went through what had become a nightly ritual since Warren died. She checked the windows, even in the bathroom, making sure that they were only open a few inches and that the safety latches were out. Then she checked the back door and was surprised to find it unlocked. She was sure she had locked it after she took out the garbage. Had Warren junior gone outside?

Undeterred by her refusal to sell the house, Warren junior had stopped by again today to insist that she be realistic about her financial situation and to tell her an appraiser and a real estate agent would be coming by. Once again, she pointed out to Warren that he was an economist at the Chicago Board of Trade. His father had been a machine operator at Johnson Motors.

Surely, if his father had managed to put him through school, he could manage to help his mother.

Had Warren junior gone outside? Then there was the appraiser. What was it about him that seemed so familiar? His eyes? He reminded her of someone. If she hadn't been so distracted because Warren junior had sent him, she might have remembered who it was. He had gone down to the basement, and yes, outside. She should have checked the door after he left. No matter, she'd lock it now. In the old house, they had never bothered to lock the door at all.

Sophia returned to the kitchen, put the kettle on, warmed the china teapot with tap water, and filled the tea ball. She buttered some crackers and arranged them on a saucer, poured the tea, took her snack to the living room, and settled into the recliner. As she reached for the book she was reading, she remembered the laundry. It would smell sour if she waited until morning. Better to take care of it now, before she got too comfortable.

Narrow stairs led to the partially finished basement. The dryer was old and the drum squeaked as it rotated. Sophia thought about waiting until tomorrow to wash the other load, but this was Wednesday and the laundry had been sorted since Monday.

She remembered the unlocked door and thought about checking the workshop and storage area, but she did not.

Later, as she dozed in the recliner, an absence of noise awakened her. The dryer had stopped. She could put the second load in and go to bed. It was after eleven. Maybe she would sleep in tomorrow. Maybe that real estate man would come early. She would not leave this house. It was not the house she had planned to live out her years in, but she had never lived in an apartment and she would not now. Warren junior knew her well enough to know that.

Sophia walked through the kitchen without turning on the light. The bathroom door was closed. She hadn't closed it. Warren must have been in there. She would have to clean the floor around the toilet tomorrow. He was a splasher. That was one of his less irritating habits. Sophia flicked on the lights to the basement. As she reached the second step, the bathroom door opened. Before she could turn around, a hard push propelled her forward.

CHAPTER 1

After the fireworks, Marti MacAlister and Ben Walker sat on the sand near the breakwater, watching as small craft navigated the narrow channel that connected the marina with Lake Michigan. Lincoln Prairie's annual Fourth of July celebration was an all-day event, with vendors' stalls and local entertainment. Marti and Ben, teamed up with Slim and Cowboy, the vice cops who shared Marti's office, and two firemen Ben worked with, had taken second place in the volleyball tournament. This was a first for Marti, socializing with the other cops. She felt self-conscious, especially when Slim called her "Big Mac" and Ben gave her a congratulatory pat on the butt. One of Ben's friends invited them to a party the following week. Marti couldn't remember the last time she had gone to a party, and she had to explain that it would depend on whether she was working a case.

Marti sat with her arms around her legs and rested her chin on her knees. The sand felt warm against the soles of her feet. Her nine-year-old son, Theo, and Ben's son,

Mike, were sprawled on a blanket beneath the pine trees, giggling as they listened to a tape of scary stories. Her fifteen-year-old daughter, Joanna, was walking on the breakwater with her boyfriend, Chris.

As Marti watched the red, green, and white running lights that blinked and bobbed against the dark outline of sky and lake, she felt more relaxed than she had in weeks. So far this year, there had been eleven homicides in Lincoln Prairie. June set a record with three, all drug- or gang-related. She and Vic, her partner, had wrapped up the last one two days ago.

Ben moved closer. "It's nice to see you having some fun for a change. You haven't had any time for yourself lately."

"Or for you, or the kids, or anyone else, except the dead."

"Are you okay with that?"

"Are you?" Marti asked. One of the advantages of being overworked was that she didn't have time to deal with this relationship, either. It was a friendship, they had both agreed last summer, as if it were some way station where she could stop and deal with certain realities, like her husband's death, and avoid certain realities, like getting on with her life. Even now that she knew how Johnny died, had even helped put his killer in jail, she was still somehow on hold.

"Are you?" Ben asked.

"No. I . . ." She shook her head. Until Ben, there had only been Johnny. She had never dated anyone else, never been intimate with anyone else. She needed to talk with Ben about that, but it wasn't an easy thing to discuss. "There's never any time these days — not for anything."

"Do you want us to spend more time together?"

She nodded. Ben chuckled.

"What's so funny?" she asked.

"Us," Ben said. "Carol and I never had this discussion. We were both in the military. I wasn't the first, or even the second. Neither was she. We were adul   ade adult decisions, or so we thou_.

"And?"

Ben reached out and caught a tendril of Marti's hair, winding it around his finger. He moved so close, she could feel his breath against her forehead.

"This is different. You expect to be courted, don't you?"

Marti thought about that for a minute. "I suppose I do."

Ben put his arms about her. "Courtship, at my age. Well, my sister won't believe it, and I can just hear my mother now. 'I told you that one day you were gonna run up against one of them women who wouldn't put up with your foolishness. Got your nose wide open, don't she?' "

Marti smiled at "nose wide open," a reference to being head over heels in love. "Do I?"

Ben grinned. "Actually, I think this urge to wake up every morning with the same warm body beside me must be some kind of revenge for the lustfulness of my youth."

"You exaggerate."

"Maybe. But I lusted in my heart all the time."

Marti rested her head against his chest, enjoying the closeness and relieved that things could stay this way for a while. She wasn't ready for anything else.

A few minutes later, Ben said, "Before I met you, when Mike and Theo first started playing together, I'd watch Theo and think, His dad is dead, just like Mike's mom is. Why isn't he getting into trouble in school? Why isn't he overeating? And then I met you, and I thought that maybe if I tried to deal with what's happened, maybe Mike would, too."

"And?"

"And I guess I agree with you. After Carol, the last time I didn't want to be alone anymore I married the first woman who said yes. It wasn't good for any of us, not her, not Mike, not me. This time, courtship sounds like a good idea. Maybe turning forty this month has something to do with it — middle age."

Marti thought of the signet ring she had ordered for him. She had even bought a card. For the first time this year, she was ready for a birthday. She turned to Ben and they kissed. She felt a sudden urgency she hadn't known since Johnny died. She pulled away. "At this rate, this might be a real short courtship," she said.

CHAPTER 2

Sophia Admunds's house was on the northeast side of town, on a bluff not far from the lake. Tall oaks shaded the quiet street, and as Marti parked across from the small bungalow, she inhaled the scent of recently cut grass. People were clustered in small groups along the sidewalk. An ambulance, a station wagon from the coroner's office, and the evidence technician's black-and-white had attracted a crowd. Marti scanned their faces, paying particular attention to a white-haired woman with a dowager's hump who stood alone and dabbed at her eyes, and to a younger woman who sat cross-legged under a birch tree. Without taking her eyes from the house, the young woman talked quietly with two little girls.

A black Lexus with the driver's door open was parked in Sophia Admunds's driveway. The driver sat sideways, talking to Marti's partner, Matthew "Vik" Jessenovik. Vik was four inches taller than Marti's five ten. He was leaning over the car, and Marti could just make out what he was saying.

17

"I'm so sorry about this, sir. Terrible thing, finding your mother like this. You are sure it's your mother?" Vik sounded concerned, but he had a way of seeming menacing even when he was not. The craggy face and beaked nose that had healed crookedly after a break were not his fault, but his scowls, sneers, and habitual grumpiness could intimidate anyone except children. "You haven't spoken to her since Wednesday, and you didn't go inside, but you're sure it's her?"

Marti couldn't hear what the man said, but Vik's wiry salt-and-pepper eyebrows almost met as he frowned.

"Well, yes, sir, I can understand why you didn't go inside. It's been hot these past few days." He paused while the man spoke. "Oh, I see. The officer over there described her hair and what she was wearing the last time you saw her —"

Vik straightened up as the man interrupted, then said, "No, sir, it shouldn't take much longer, and yes, you can leave soon." Vik spoke with just a touch of annoyance. "She is your mother, and we do want to know what happened to her, so try to be a little patient. Do you think you could come to the precinct tomorrow? Maybe about eleven? Just in case we have any odd details we need to clear up. I'd sure appreciate that, sir. Here's my card."

Marti looked at the uniform standing just outside the front door and nodded toward the Lexus. "The woman's son?"

"Yes ma'am. Warren Admunds, Jr., Ph.D. He says he called her yesterday and didn't get any answer, came over this morning, opened the door, got a whiff of the smell, and called us. Looks like she's been dead a couple of days."

"Find out who those people are." Marti indicated the older woman and the woman with the little girls.

Vik came over as Marti was taking a small jar of Vick's VapoRub out of her purse.

"Says he's late for work. We're talking about his mother and he can't wait to leave."

Marti rubbed the ointment in her nostrils to mask the smell, handed the jar to Vik, and went inside.

In less than a minute, Vik was standing at the door leading to the basement, calling instructions to the evidence tech. "And what's that on the step?" he said, sounding irritable and impatient at the same time. "Did you see that dark spot there on the second step?"

"We'll be out of here in a few minutes, Jessenovik," a male voice called. "You'll get our report."

"I don't want your report; I want to know

what's on the step."

"In due time."

After the body was removed, one of the technicians spoke to Marti.

Ignoring Vik, he said, "That's oil on the step. There're traces of it on both of the woman's shoes, none that I could see on her clothing."

Marti touched the step with the tip of her finger and sniffed. "It isn't motor oil," she said. That smell was stronger than the Vick's. "And I don't think it's machine oil, either. Cooking oil, maybe. Let me know if you find anything else."

She looked around the basement: a workshop with tools organized beneath a workbench and hanging from nails on the wall; a laundry area with clothes wet and sour-smelling in the washer, another load that was dry; a storeroom with cobwebs and dusty boxes.

The four upstairs rooms were crowded with old heavy oak and mahogany furniture intended for a much larger place. Bric-a-brac and photographs seemed to cover every surface in the living room and bedroom — all the objects recently dusted and, Marti thought, important. There were several photographs of a woman wearing her hair in a bun at the nape of her neck, the same hairstyle as the deceased's; an enlargement of an informal picnic shot with two laughing children; and an old black-and-white formal photo with four solemn youngsters grouped around an unsmiling woman. Marti scanned the woman's face. There was a sternness in her expression, a rigidity in the set of her spine. The children in the picnic scene were leaning away from the woman. Two of the children in the black-and-white photo, a boy and a girl who seemed close in age, were touching. The others were not.

Marti walked a narrow path on an Oriental rug between overstuffed chairs and oversized tables, all in excellent condition, protected with antimacassars and crocheted pineapple doilies. A Tiffany lamp beside the recliner was on, the light shining through multicolored glass. An open book lay facedown on the carpet. Wednesday's *News-Times* had been refolded, with sale items in the food section circled in red. Who would have taken Sophia Admunds shopping? Had she planned to spend the Fourth of July with her family? Marti looked at the photographs again. Had the old woman lived a full life, or had a life filled with things?

"Ma'am," the tech said. "We found this in the garbage." He held up a plastic bag with a dish towel inside. "It's got oil on it."

"Thanks. Fax your reports as soon as they're ready. Maybe we can get a quick

21

closure on this. Looks like she slipped and fell down the stairs."

Marti went to the front porch. Vik followed. "At least this one was considerate and we didn't get called here on a holiday or in the middle of the night," he said.

Three boys on bicycles slowed as they pedaled past.

"Geez, the old tattletale's dead," the smallest one said. "I told you guys to stop taking the lids off her garbage cans to bait the raccoons."

"Oh, that didn't kill her. Come on. Race you home!"

Marti took a deep breath. The perfume of a nearby rosebush didn't quite chase away the smell of Vick's, but the odor of death was gone. She wiped sweat from her forehead. It had been stuffy inside, and the air outside was hot. Leaves rustled overhead, but the breeze blew warm, not cool. Marti's back was damp. She was wearing a short-sleeved jacket that concealed the weapon holstered at her hip. Since coming to Lincoln Prairie, she most often kept her gun in her purse, but the cases she had been working on for the past month were more like those she had worked in Chicago, involving drug dealers and gangs, so she had switched to a holster.

A car turned the corner and slowed as it approached. Marti stared at the bearded driver until he looked away. She watched the car turn into a driveway several houses down. This was an older neighborhood. Unlike the newer subdivisions with small lots and four models to choose from, these homes had been here for years and no two were alike. Sophia Admunds's bungalow squatted comfortably between a two-story colonial with window boxes of ivy and red petunias and a sprawling split-level brick ranch.

Marti walked to the driveway. The Lexus was gone. Warren Admunds wouldn't have to go to the coroner's office to identify the remains. That would be done through X rays and dental records. She walked around to the low picket fence that enclosed the backyard. Two Chinese maples shaded the small lot. There was no garage. She returned to the porch.

"Hell of a summer so far," Vik said. He wiped sweat from his forehead with a rumpled handkerchief.

"It looks like things are getting back to normal. This was probably just an accident."

"It's about time. We've had gang hits, drive-bys, domestic homicides. It's that nuclear plant in Zion. It's emitting something that's affecting the lunatic fringe. They never should have built those things so close to civilization."

"Burnout," Marti said. One day off hadn't been enough. They needed a real vacation. "Let's talk with the neighbors."

They spoke to the woman with the children first. "I'm Lynn Stallings," she said. "I live two houses down. We can talk on the deck."

A blanket was spread on the grass and the two girls, who looked to be about five and six, were playing with dolls.

"I didn't see Mrs. Admunds at all yesterday. She was in that house dead, wasn't she?" the woman said.

Vik gave a noncommittal shrug, indicating that he wanted Marti to ask the questions.

"Did you know her very well?" Marti asked.

"No. We spoke, passed the time of day. She asked me to bring the girls over for milk and cookies, but I never had time. And she was old. If the girls had become attached to her, and now this, it would be much too difficult for them to deal with."

Marti wasn't sure she agreed. Sophia Admunds might have been lonely. She might have enjoyed having children around. "When's the last time you saw her?"

"Wednesday evening, sitting on the porch. I noticed last night when we came back from watching the fireworks that the light was still on in her living room, but I didn't

24

think anything was wrong."

"Have you noticed anything unusual in the neighborhood lately?"

The woman looked at her for a minute. "Are you saying this wasn't . . . a heart attack or something?"

"We don't know. Right now, this is just routine."

"Oh. Well, no. We have a neighborhood watch that works. Nobody speeds, nobody solicits, and nobody breaks in. No barking dogs, no loud music after ten. And there's a block party the first Saturday in August."

Neda Wagner, the older woman who lived across the street, stopped pinching back petunias and pulling up weeds to talk with the detectives. Marti could see Vik resisting the urge to help the woman as she got to her feet. "So, now Sophia is gone. What was it, her heart?"

"Did she have heart trouble, ma'am?" Marti asked.

"No. She didn't have a thing more wrong with her than I have with me. We're just getting old, that's all. Even when you're not sick, things wear out, quit working."

"When's the last time you saw her?"

"Sophia came over and we had lunch together Wednesday afternoon. I saw her sitting on the porch toward dark."

"How did she seem?"

"Oh, she was a little upset, that's all."

"Why?"

"An appraiser had come to look at the house, and a real estate agent was coming by, too. Her children wanted her to move into an apartment."

"How did she feel about that?"

"How would you feel?"

Marti thought about all of Sophia Admunds's furniture and memorabilia. "How long had she lived here?"

"About seven years. Warren had already had several strokes when they moved in. He died a year later. She always thought the move was what killed him, not being around what was familiar. They used to live in a big old Victorian on Garden Place."

And having culled furnishings and belongings from that house, Marti thought, Sophia Admunds had been expected to choose among her possessions again.

"Such a shame," the old woman said. "You spend all those years saving up for your retirement, just the two of you; you make all those plans about what you're going to do, where you're going to go. Work all your life and by the time you're able to live for yourself, you're either too old or too sick, or you just up and die, like Warren and my Joe."

"Was she depressed about having to move?" Marti asked.

"Oh, Sophia had no intentions of moving."

"Why not?"

"Look around you. Would you give this up to live in some senior citizens' high-rise surrounded with old people and concrete? Especially if you were neither sickly nor senile?"

"Do you know why her son wanted her to move?"

"To make her money last longer. You know how kids are these days. They're always afraid they're going to have to take care of you."

It was after five o'clock by the time Marti and Vik finished talking with the neighbors. Apparently, Neda Wagner was the only close friend Sophia Admunds had. They returned to her house and went through the dust-covered boxes in the basement. Everything in them was old, and as far as Marti could tell, irrelevant to the woman's death.

Back at the precinct, Marti spoke with Sophia Admunds's doctor while Vik went through the preliminary reports.

"No significant health problems," she said when she hung up.

"No unusual police reports in that area," Vik said. "No strangers, repairmen, or con artists. No forced entry into the house. No indications she had or was planning to have any guests."

"And oil on the second step leading to the basement," Marti added. The autopsy was scheduled for the next day and the coroner's jury would meet the following Wednesday. She expected a ruling of accidental death.

CHAPTER 3

Marti got up early Saturday morning and attended the Admunds autopsy. She and Vik had agreed to alternate autopsy attendance, at least for the summer, and it was her turn. In Chicago, she had seldom had time for autopsies. Here, they were part of the job. Sometimes, like today, she felt a quiet outrage that someone could live so long and experience such indignities at death.

When she got to the precinct, Vik was there, along with Slim and Cowboy.

"Big Mac," Cowboy said. "Had breakfast yet?"

Admunds had been in that house dead for two days. The thought of food made her stomach churn.

Slim started toward her and she waved him away. The odor of Obsession for Men combined with the smell of fresh brewed coffee would be enough to make her vomit.

Cowboy smiled at her as he selected a chocolate-covered bismarck from a bakery box beside the coffeepot. He squeezed it until custard popped out. "Like popping a pimple," he said.

"Okay," Marti said. "If I throw up, I'm aiming for your desk."

"Yes, ma'am." A glob of custard plopped on the floor as he headed for the door.

Slim reached into the box, bit into a doughnut, and held it up so she could see the jelly. "Hah, I gutted the damned thing!" Grinning, he left right behind Cowboy.

"Mrs. Admunds died of a broken neck," Marti said as soon as they were gone. "The medical examiner says she went down the steps headfirst and landed facedown. There was a new bruise about the size of a half-dollar on her left shoulder."

"Could she have gotten the bruise in the fall?"

"It's possible, but since she didn't go down the steps feetfirst or land on her back, it doesn't seem likely. It looks like she was pushed."

"Anything else?"

"Not really. She was in good health, just the usual signs of aging."

"So why was the oil on the step? So we'd think she slipped and fell?"

"There were traces on the soles of her shoes. It was there before she fell."

"Premeditation?" Vik said.

"Sounds like it to me."

"When did she die?"

"Sometime after she was seen at seven-thirty by the neighbor and four the next morning."

"The lamp by the chair was on. And it looked like she had been reading. I'd guess it was earlier rather than later."

Warren Admunds showed up at ten minutes to eleven. He was of average height and wore a monogrammed tennis shirt and navy slacks. His deep tan made his gray eyes seem pale. Marti tried not to stare at the top of his head. He had let the hair above his left ear grow long enough to cover the bald spot. The thin brown hair combed across his white scalp had separated in a striped effect that Marti was sure was unintentional.

Warren looked at Marti, then chose the chair nearest Vik. Marti wondered why he didn't buy a toupee.

"Good to see you, sir," Vik said, coming from behind his desk and looking everywhere but at Admunds' head as he pulled up a chair and sat facing him. "Now, Mr. Admunds, could you tell me exactly what happened at your mother's house yesterday?"

Admunds looked down at his hands, then at Vik. "I, um, I went by the house. When I opened the door . . ." He shuddered. "God."

"And you did not go inside at all?"

"No. I . . . no."

"Tell me about the last time you saw your mother."

"She was . . . okay."

"Had you disagreed about anything recently? Was there anything that she might have been upset about?"

Admunds's Adam's apple bobbed as he swallowed. "The house. We needed to sell the house. It was far beyond what she could afford for more than a few more years. She didn't want to move again. I could understand that, but . . . it wasn't realistic." He took a deep breath. "What has to be done has to be done. There was no point in putting it off any longer."

"Did she disagree with you about this?" Vik asked.

"Yes, but not on Wednesday. I just stopped by to tell her that the real estate agent and an appraiser would be coming by."

"How long were you there?"

"Maybe ten minutes."

"How was your mother when you left?"

"Angry, but okay." Warren wrung his hands. "Look, I have houseguests. I really have to go."

"Your mother, sir," Vik said. "She's dead. Speaking of which, would you mind telling me where you were between seven o'clock Wednesday night and four A.M. Thursday morning?"

Admunds stared at him for a minute. "At home," he said, swallowing. "With my wife."

"Do you have brothers and sisters, sir?"

"What?"

"Family," Vik said.

"Oh, yes. Of course."

"Could we have their names and addresses?"

"The wake is tomorrow. They'll be there."

Vik took out his pad.

Warren smoothed the hair on the top of his head. "Okay. My brother lives in Champaign."

"Sisters, sir?"

"Nadya's in California and Jori lives in Arizona. They'll be here tomorrow."

"Addresses and phone numbers, sir?"

Vik wrote that down and closed his notebook. "Thank you, sir."

"That's all?"

"Yes. For now."

Vik rubbed his chin. Marti nodded. There wasn't much point in asking Admunds anything else until they had more information.

As soon as the door to their office closed, Vik looked at Marti. "Interesting, isn't it, the questions he didn't ask?"

"Eager to get here, find out what we know, but no curiosity at all," Marti agreed.

"And," Vik said, "no signs of forced entry at his mother's house."

By one o'clock, they knew that the substance on the step was cooking oil, and the dish towel had the same oil on it. The only other odd bit of evidence was a clump of tan clay that wasn't consistent with anything found near the house.

"Tech says it looks like it had dried in the tread of a tennis shoe and came loose," Vik said. "Looks like it's time we began introducing ourselves to some of the other members of the family."

Half an hour later, they were heading for Champaign.

"Damned toll collectors," Vik complained as they idled half a mile from the tollbooth and inched their way forward. "You'd think one of them would be smart enough to leave the gate up and let everyone just throw in their money. So what if they get short-changed. You read the newspapers lately? They're making money hand over fist and even letting some of it trickle down to their peons."

Once they were on Interstate 57, the traffic thinned and farmland, interspersed with small towns and truck stops, dominated the landscape.

Vik identified the types of farms by smell. "Cows," he said, then, "Slaughterhouse," then, "Roll up the windows. Pigs."

One whiff and Marti decided that cows

34

were the least offensive.

Champaign was a sprawling college town. Warren Admunds's brother, Gilbert, lived in a neighborhood much like his mother's, in a big old wood-frame house painted yellow. It had a swing and two wicker rockers with plump yellow cushions on the porch. Honeysuckle grew along a picket fence. On one side of the house, toward the back, three little boys, the oldest not more than seven, played on a combination swing set and playhouse. As Marti watched, the tallest boy swung on a rope ladder and jumped into the sandbox.

"Dare you!" he called. The younger boys ignored him. "Double dare you!" There were no takers.

A woman holding a baby came to the front door as Marti and Vik negotiated a walkway cluttered with tricycles, bicycles, and a Big Wheel.

"Watch it with these toys," Vik muttered to Marti. "If you break your leg, I've forgotten how to put on a splint."

"Can I help you?" the woman said when they got close enough.

"We'd like to speak with Gilbert Admunds," Vik said.

The woman glanced behind her. "Is it important? He's a little upset. His mother just passed away."

"That's what we want to see him about,"

35

Vik said. They showed her their shields.

"Police?"

"It's just routine, ma'am."

She hesitated, then held the door open. Inside, the air was cool. Toys were scattered everywhere and a playpen with a clown mobile was set up in the living room. Marti picked up a blanket, clean diaper, and bottle from the couch and put them on the table so they could sit down. A short, thin man came in a few minutes later. He was balding like his brother but had made no attempt to disguise it, at least not today. He sighed as he sat across from them.

"I didn't know that police officers from one jurisdiction would come to another because of something like this." He looked from Marti to Vik, then spoke to Vik. "Warren said Ma was alone. . . ." He wiped at his eyes. "Sorry. There isn't anything wrong, is there? I mean . . . Warren said it was quick, that she didn't suffer. He was too busy to talk, but I assumed that she had a heart attack or stroke or something."

When they didn't respond, Gilbert Admunds said, "Did someone break in? Did they hurt her? My God, what happened? Why are you here?" His voice kept rising as he spoke. "I just can't . . . she would have been here that night if it hadn't been Warren's turn to have her over for the holiday. They must have argued again. He could

36

have told me. She should have called. That's all she had to do, just call me, and she would have been here, not alone."

The woman returned without the baby, sat down, and put her arm around Gilbert's shoulders. "This is my wife," he said. "She was alone, Ellen, alone."

Ellen patted his back, much as she might soothe a child. "Whatever happened, it's over," she said. She gave Marti and Vik a hard stare. "At least for your mom." She turned to Vik. "Why are you here?"

Marti spoke. "Your mother was found at the foot of the steps in the basement. It wasn't a heart attack."

"Then what?" the woman asked. "Did she fall?"

"How was her health?" Marti asked. "Did she ever complain about anything?"

"Not about any health problems."

The woman's tone implied that there might have been other complaints.

"Poor Mom," Gilbert said. "She was finally able just to take life easy, and this happens."

As he spoke, his wife moved away from him. "What did happen?" she asked.

"She fell down a flight of stairs and broke her neck," Marti said, looking from one to the other to gauge their reaction. Gilbert covered his eyes. His wife sat with her lips pressed together. "Did someone . . .

was it . . . an accident?"

"Were there any problems recently?" Marti asked. "Any conflict with the neighbors?"

"No," Gilbert said. "That was one of the things she liked about the neighborhood. The people kept pretty much to themselves, but there was always someone to cut the grass or shovel the snow or make some minor repair — things I would have done if I lived closer."

"And Warren?"

"No time," Gilbert said. "New wife, new house. If only I could have found a teaching position closer to home. I should have accepted something at the junior college. I could have been there."

"Where was she going to live after the house was sold?" Marti asked.

"Oh, that," Ellen said. "She would never have allowed that to happen. Gil was worried because there wasn't much we could do to help out financially. But I told him, as stubborn as she is, she'll never agree to go anywhere else as long as she's able to care for herself. And Warren is in a position to help her."

"I wanted her to come here," Gilbert said, "live with us, but she didn't want to leave Lincoln Prairie."

His wife stood and moved to the window.

"There's plenty of room here," Gilbert

said. "Ellen inherited this place from her father."

Ellen clenched her hands into fists but didn't say anything. Marti wondered how mother-in-law and daughter-in-law got along.

"And you don't know of any problems, any disagreements your mother might have had recently?"

"You can't think someone did this deliberately, that someone pushed her down the stairs? Nobody would do that, not to my mother."

Marti glanced at Ellen. The expression on her face suggested otherwise.

"I suppose that sounds stupid these days," Gilbert said. "Thinking nobody would hurt a harmless old woman who never did anything to anybody. Nowadays, it's like the lottery. Who knows when somebody will get you, and for no reason at all."

His wife folded her arms and leaned against the window as she gnawed on the corner of her lip.

Marti and Vik stopped for dinner and headed east to Lincoln Prairie at just the right time to get stalled at the tollgates again.

"Too bad the wife wasn't home alone when we got there," Marti said. "Her husband might have thought his mother was a saint, but she sure didn't."

"The wake's tomorrow," Vik said. "And we still have to talk with the sisters."

"And maybe both wives," Marti said, "without their husbands."

"Interesting how one son is all upset and the other doesn't seem to give a damn."

Marti thought of the stern-faced woman captured in the photo, in tones of black and white. "Even if she wasn't such a sweet old lady, that doesn't mean one of them would kill her."

"Yeah, but they're our best suspects right now, and if one of her sons didn't do it, that leaves us with a cast of thousands. We have to find out how important selling that house was. Money's a great motive for just about anything."

As she drove, Marti considered Warren, then Gilbert. Had one of them pushed Sophia Admunds down those stairs? She had seen one family member killed by another so often, she wondered how she could still find the idea difficult to accept. She didn't know enough about either of the Admunds sons yet. Was Warren's attitude and behavior a denial of grief or an indication of guilt? Which sister was standing near her brother in the photograph? Was she younger or older? Would they draw close now, or had time and separation created distance? The real question was their capacity to plan to kill. That oil said premeditation. This was not an impulsive action. Somebody had thought about killing Sophia Admunds, decided how it would happen, and carried out their plan. Cold-blooded? Perhaps. Or perhaps the result of a great deal of emotion.

CHAPTER 4

When Marti and Vik returned to Sophia Admunds's house late Sunday morning, a tall, angular woman opened the door. She was dressed in khaki shorts and a man's shirt. Her straight shoulder-length hair swung as she moved. Marti tried to place her in the old photograph but could not.

"Police, ma'am," Vik said as they showed her their shields. "Sorry to bother you, but if it's all right, we'd like to have another look around. We need to go through everything in the storage room again."

The woman extended her hand to both of them. "I'm Jori Yolen. Come on in."

Inside, packing boxes sat on the sofa and chairs. More were stacked against a wall. The bric-a-brac on the tables looked as if it was being sorted. Jori Yolen gestured toward it. "I've got a short leave of absence, but Mother had so much stuff."

"We've processed everything here that we need to," Vik said. "But please don't remove anything yet."

The pictures that had hung on the wall were stacked in a corner. Squatting, Marti sorted through them until she found the two that had caught her attention.

"Those are Nadya's children," Jori said when she looked at the color photograph. "Very outspoken, both of them. My mother disapproved." Taking the other, she smiled. "Mother hated having her picture taken, but Daddy insisted. Nadya and Warren were so close then. Nadya can't make it in time for the wake. She'll be here tomorrow."

"Have you found anything unusual among your mother's possessions?" Marti asked. So far, she hadn't been able to identify anything of importance among the woman's personal effects.

Jori gave her an appraising look. "Why don't I fix us all a cup of coffee?"

The same sorting process was taking place in the kitchen. Three counters were stacked with sets of dishes. Each looked like a service for twelve.

Jori picked up a saucer. "My grandmother brought these from Poland."

Vik went over to take a closer look.

"You said your name's Jessenovik? You're Polish, too," Jori said.

Vik nodded.

"Warren wants to sell all of this. I'd like to say it'll go cheap, but . . ." She shrugged. "Knowing Warren . . ."

Jori poured mugs of hot coffee and made a space on the table. "Now according to

Warren, Mother lost her balance and fell down the stairs. According to Gilbert, somebody pushed her, and the most obvious choice is Warren."

Marti stirred her coffee and said nothing.

"Someone has to deal with this, and as usual, as the oldest, everyone expects it to be me. So I've told Warren, Gilbert, and Nadya to be completely forthcoming when you speak with them. As for your question . . ." She paused to measure two level teaspoons of sugar into her cup. "I have been going through Mother's belongings with an eye to finding something odd. I haven't gotten to the boxes in the basement yet, but so far, there's nothing."

Marti decided to be direct. "How was Warren's relationship with your mother?"

"Warren is a prissy pain in the ass, except when it comes to women. He's finally outdone himself and met up with some little bimbo who hopefully will take him for everything he's got so the rest of us can convince him that he's still mortal."

"Why did he want your mother to sell this house?"

She thought for a minute. "I've wondered about that, too. Gilbert really doesn't have enough income to help out, but I'm an attorney and Nadya's a pediatrician. We were more than willing to step in. In fact, I specifically told Warren not to pursue this any

44

further. Now Gilbert tells me that Warren had an appraiser and a Realtor coming in."

She aligned a spoon beside the mug, her expression severe. "So at the moment, I don't know what is going on with Warren, but I will find out."

Jori Yolen's candor didn't surprise Marti as much as the fact that she was an attorney. Marti respected most lawyers, trusted few. What kind of a game was this one playing? How much would Jori tell them if she did find out the truth and it implicated one of her brothers?

Looking around the room, Marti noticed an ornate soup tureen. "Did that come from Poland, too?" she asked.

Jori nodded. "Just about everything in this house belonged to my grandmother. Daddy could never have afforded any of it. My mother married for love, and she did love him. It broke her heart when he died. She was never the same after that."

The woman in the photographs didn't seem to have changed much over the years. "Did you grow up in your grandmother's house?"

"Why, yes. Beautiful place, but none of us wanted to live there. It was like living in a museum."

"I suppose it will be difficult, deciding who gets what."

Jori made a face. "We dusted and polished

45

this stuff. We were never allowed to sit on any of the furniture. This table was in the dining room and used exclusively for guests until Mother brought it here. I've never eaten on those dishes. Once a year, when her sister and brother were still living, Mother took out one set on Christmas Eve along with the silver. The children ate in the kitchen on melanine. None of us wants anything to do with any of it."

"What was your mother like before your father died?"

"She wasn't . . . demonstrative, but she was fiercely proud and protective of all of us. She was a good mother. Mass and Communion every Sunday. Hot meals every day. When we were little, she read to us and listened to our prayers at bedtime. She sang to us in Polish, and her cooking was delicious. She taught Jori and me to cook. She volunteered at school. She liked being a mother and a wife."

"And afterward?"

Jori got up and spent several minutes fussing over a second cup of coffee and adding more to their half-filled cups. "She was angry, I think. Until then, life had pretty much gone her way. And she was . . . something troubled her. I was never sure what. I thought maybe she blamed herself somehow, but she took such good care of him. She became very quiet, very remote afterward, almost reclusive."

"Attorney Yolen, in your opinion, would either of your brothers —"

"Push my mother down a flight of stairs? Nice choice of titles, Detective. I appreciate that." She rested her chin on the tips of her fingers for a minute, then rearranged her spoon. "As we both know, in a moment of passion, anger, anything can happen. If you think this was premeditated, then I would have to say no."

Marti wasn't sure she agreed with that. A lot depended on how much pressure either man was under, and what kind. "I appreciate your candor."

Jori smiled. "As you have reminded me, I, too, am an officer of the court. Besides, I've prosecuted enough cases to know that obstruction only serves to obscure the truth. If my mother's death wasn't accidental, then I want you find out what happened just as much as you do. And based on your approach, I'm inclined to think that you will take the time to find out, and apprehend the right person."

"And if that is a family member?"

"Then we shall see."

"What did you think of her?" Vik said as Marti drove to the precinct.

"I liked her."

"Me, too."

"But I don't trust her. You haven't been able to talk with that appraiser yet?"

"He's out of town until next week."

Marti resisted an impatient urge to bring Warren in for questioning, before his lawyer sister had the opportunity to provide counsel. Until they knew more about the oil and the dirt, she would remain cautious. "Motive," she said. "Unless we can break down an alibi, this one will come down to why."

CHAPTER 5

It was almost midnight when Liddy Fields changed into her swimsuit. The motel was usually quiet on Sunday, but tonight the bar was crowded, and sailors were unpredictable drunks. The cabana, too fancy a name for a place in need of paint, was dark except for the light that came from the windows at the far end of the room. Barefoot, she avoided the wet places on the concrete floor. The air was warm and moist and vapor rose from the still water that reflected the blue of the rectangular pool. Liddy tested the water with her toes, then, bracing herself for the sudden chill, sat on the edge at the deep end, up to her knees in the cold.

Sitting there, she remembered the ocean, always cold, no matter how hot the day was. As a child, she went to the beach all summer. Momma couldn't swim and wouldn't let her go in the water higher than her waist. While her momma floated, eyes closed and belly up, she got the other kids to teach her to swim. She wasn't sure if she'd gone to the beach as often as she thought she had, but summer, sunshine, sand, and ice-cold salty water all flowed together in her mind.

She hadn't seen the Atlantic in over twenty years. She felt as if she had traveled thousands of miles to get . . . to get where? This room was small and the motel old. Rain from an afternoon thunderstorm had settled in a puddle where the roof dipped, and she could hear a slow, steady drip. With two drooping artificial palm trees inside, and the multicolored plastic lanterns that hung outside the windows, she couldn't even close her eyes and pretend she was at the beach.

Liddy let her legs rise to the surface until she could see her toes, then lowered them into the water again. Sometimes, years ago, Momma would let her go into the old aquarium. Huge sea turtles in square tanks would float from top to bottom again and again because they had no place else to go. Neither did she. It seemed as if she had come such a long way to get here. She wouldn't be going anywhere else.

The tile walls muffled the tinny sounds of a cheap band. Glass broke. A fight? Her staff was supposed to card the young sailors who came here, but sometimes, when she wasn't there to make sure . . . The door to the pool room opened. A woman took a step in and saw Liddy. "Oops. Not in here, sweetie." The young man standing behind her pulled her back into the hall, leaving the door ajar.

The music grew louder. Liddy thought about closing the door. Instead, she concentrated on the drumbeats until an echo throbbed in her head. Then she slipped into the pool.

The smell and taste of chlorine chased her memories away. Would she ever smell or taste salt water again? She swam with swift, sure strokes, knowing with her eyes closed when she approached the perimeters of the pool and feeling like a seal as she turned. She swam without tiring, although it had been a long day. She swam until she felt one with the water, exuberant, even young. She was smiling when she felt a hand grasp her ankle. She flailed her arms and grabbed for the surface. She could not get her head above water.

Twenty miles away, Alma Miller thrashed at the force that restrained her. Fingers, tight as a vise, were clamped around her ankle. Water. She couldn't breathe. But she had to. Her chest. Pain. Water — in her mouth, her throat, water.

"No-o-o. No-o-o."

Alma sat up all at once, trembling with cold and gasping for breath.

"Alma? Another dream?" Darred asked.

"Cold," Alma said. Her teeth were chattering. "So cold."

Darred sat up. "It's okay. You're here. With me."

He went to the closet for a blanket and put it around her shoulders. Alma leaned against her husband, felt his arms strong around her.

"Water," she said. "I couldn't get out of the water."

She shuddered again. Sometimes she didn't know what the dreams meant.

CHAPTER 6

As Marti squatted beside the woman's body, she resisted an impulse to brush long wet strands of kinky gray hair from her forehead. The muscles in the woman's face were stiff with early rigor. Marti dipped her hand in the water. Cold. The rigor had been slowed by the water temperature. She glanced at her watch. Several hours had passed since a guest taking an early-morning swim had dived in and seen the body at the bottom of the pool. Paramedics had been called, then the police. They were still waiting for someone from the coroner's office. Vik had requested Dr. Cyprian, their favorite pathologist, but he was in court.

"Then get him out of there," Vik yelled into the phone. "Now! I want him here now!"

The victim, Liddy Fields, wasn't a guest, according to the desk clerk. Liddy managed the place for the owner, lived here, went for a swim just about every night.

There were pouches of fat on the woman's upper arms, and cellulite thickened her thighs. She hadn't been in the water long enough for her fingernails to fall off, and they were painted a bright red. There was a birthmark on her neck, kidney-shaped and a darker shade of brown than her skin. Her death was neither gentle nor kind. Drowning, unless the victim was unconscious when she went into the water, was a violent, painful way to go.

Vik stooped at the edge of the pool and skimmed the surface with his fingers. He flicked water in Marti's direction.

"This is great. We can fill out the reports and file them on this one. One good thing about drownings, they're almost always accidental." He smiled. "And there's almost always no way to prove it when they're not. She had a stroke maybe, or a heart attack. Seizure, even."

"Take a look at her ankle," Marti said.

"Bruises. So what? The steps going into the pool are right there. Her arms and legs were dangling down, and her foot probably banged against the steps."

Dr. Cyprian arrived and began to examine the body.

"This one's an accident," Vik told him. "Period."

On the way out of the pool area, Vik said, "Cyprian's a sensible man. He won't be fooled by a bruise."

The Ship's Out Motel was located on the far southeast side of Lincoln Prairie, not far from the navy base, in an area that catered to sailors. Bars, pool halls, several other motels, a cleaners, record shop, and half a dozen fast-food places lined several streets just outside the military installation. Twenty-three of the twenty-eight rooms in the Ship's Out were vacant.

"We're booked full Friday to Sunday," the day clerk explained. "The rest of the week, we get mostly transients."

None of the rooms near Liddy Fields's room or the swimming pool was occupied. Marti and Vik questioned the occupants of the other rooms. All were women. One had found the body.

"I'm from Omaha," she said. "I'm here visiting my fiancé." She hugged herself as she spoke, then rubbed her arms as if she was cold. "After I was in the pool . . . I saw her. I didn't . . . she wasn't . . . she was near the bottom. She wasn't . . . I got out . . . ran. Mind if I smoke?" She retrieved a lit cigarette from an ashtray and took several deep drags. Her blond hair was still damp and she had put a T-shirt on over her bathing suit. She looked about twenty.

"I came here for my fiancé's graduation. He just got out of boot camp." She looked around the room and shuddered. "I was going to stay here for a week." Two suitcases on the bed indicated that she had changed her mind.

"Had you ever seen her before you found

her in the pool?" Marti asked.

"At the desk, when I checked in. She told me it might be a little noisy around here over the weekend but that come Monday, I'd practically have the place to myself."

"Were there any fights, arguments?"

"No. A lot of noise, but everyone was just having a good time."

Vik had checked, and there hadn't been any calls to the police.

Marti was helping herself to coffee when the clerk who worked the desk at night arrived. He was young and skinny, with stringy brown hair tied in a ponytail. "Last time I saw her was about nine-fifteen," he said. "Sunday's always quiet, and that excuse for a band they hired to bring the sailors in wasn't worth nothing."

"How do you know it was nine-fifteen?" Marti asked.

"About nine-fifteen. Liddy usually spent Sunday night in her room watching TV, but we had a couple of sailors in the bar spoiling for a fight. She stuck around until one of them left. Clock said nine-ten, but it's always off."

"Did she ask the sailors to leave?" Marti asked.

"No. We let 'em alone unless they get to fighting. Saying something just eggs 'em on."

"Would she have gone to the pool then?"

"No. She always waited until the pool closed at eleven to swim. She swam every night, unless she was sick. She . . ." He wiped his eyes with the back of his hand. "She was just . . ." His voice faltered. "She was just nice . . . you know. . . ."

Dr. Cyprian came to the lobby and called them to one side.

"An accident?" Vik said.

Cyprian shook his head.

Vik scowled. "Because of those bruises, I suppose."

"Yes," Cyprian agreed. "That, and her ankle's broken. I can't call it officially, but it looks like someone pulled her under and held on."

"Damn!" Vik threw his Styrofoam cup in a wastebasket.

The evidence tech was packing up when Marti and Vik reached Liddy's room.

"Nothing," he said.

The air smelled musty, as if the windows hadn't been opened in a while. An arrangement of flowers with lots of baby's breath and tendrils of curly pink ribbons was on a table by the window. The pink and white carnations were dying. A fat fantailed goldfish swam in the sunlight. The bowl was small and round, with no air pump or filter, just multicolored gravel and shells at the bottom. Marti sprinkled in some food as she surveyed the room.

She observed an unmade bed, a love seat, an overstuffed chair near the table. There was a view of the alley. Laundry had been sorted into two piles. In an alcove, a hot plate rested on the counter, a refrigerator beneath. The walls were a shade of blue that reminded Marti of Lake Michigan on a hot day. Stars made of silver paper were glued to the ceiling.

Vik pulled a suitcase from under the bed and opened it. It was filled with envelopes, newspaper clippings, and photographs. "Eureka," he said, but without his usual enthusiasm for documents and reports.

Marti went over to the bureau drawers, where wrinkled, rough-dried clothes had been tossed helter-skelter.

As she and Vik prepared to leave Liddy Fields's room an hour later, they didn't know much more about her than they knew when they arrived. The photographs were not recent, were not dated, and only in a few could they be reasonably certain they were looking at Fields. Most of the newspaper clippings were yellow with age. They found no insurance policy, no will, no personal correspondence except for a chain letter promising health and prosperity if copies were sent to ten friends and disaster if they were not.

In addition to Social Security, Liddy received a small pension from the state of

Rhode Island and dividends from Ameritech. Her income was not enough to live on without working. There was a savings passbook with no entries, no bank statements, no key to or receipt for a safe-deposit box.

Liddy's possessions had been expensive, but the leather shoes and purses were worn, as were the two coats. The Pendleton chesterfield was threadbare at the pockets and cuffs, and the lining in the London Fog was beginning to shred. She had two watches with gold bands and assorted rings and earrings, nothing cheap.

"So," Vik said. "We've got another dead lady, no motive — doesn't look like whoever did it took time to rob her — no relatives, no friends, no next of kin." He shifted the suitcase from one hand to the other. "Most people, when they get to be a certain age, at least stop to think that one day they might be checking out of here. Damned inconsiderate, leaving nothing." He checked his watch. "And we missed Sophia Admunds's funeral."

Marti picked up the goldfish bowl and cradled it in her arms. Looking up, she wondered who had glued the stars to the ceiling.

Nobody at the motel wanted the goldfish. Marti stopped by her house and left the bowl on the table with a note to Theo. She and Vik spent the afternoon trying to get a lead on Liddy Fields.

"Thanks," Marti said. "Send it to her in care of the county morgue." She cursed under her breath as she hung up the phone. "Well, Liddy Fields did file an income-tax return for last year, but if she has or ever had a spouse or dependents, they are not at liberty to say. However, they did agree to forward a request for that information. Let's give this to Missing Persons and see what they can track down. Their sources might be better than ours."

"Too bad the motel owner didn't demand references," Vik said. "Damned peculiar — no relatives, no friends. Worked there almost two years and nobody even knows where she came from."

"Maybe once we get whatever information Social Security has —"

"Maybe, MacAlister. People who don't want anybody knowing anything about them usually succeed. The question is, What is it that she didn't want anybody to know?"

Marti went through the slim stack of newspaper clippings again. Many were from the travel section — articles on Maine, Cape Cod, the Green Mountains, the Florida Keys, Hawaii. Others followed cases involving child abuse or missing children, some recent, some going back twenty years. Not all of the cases happened in Illinois.

"We need a vacation," Vik said. "I'd settle for a long weekend with the family."

Marti closed the file of clippings and shoved it to the far side of her desk. "Maybe next month. Maybe next year. Maybe." She took a sip of coffee — cold, just like this case. She poured the coffee in the spider plant's pot.

"Marti, I thought we agreed we were going to give it water from now on. It thrives on caffeine. Increasing and multiplying like everything else around here — robbery, murder . . ."

"You're still feeding it!"

Vik checked his watch. "Maybe we should check out the action at the Ship's Out Motel. It's about time for the boys from the base to start barhopping."

The band playing at the motel *was* awful. By the time the bar closed, Marti never wanted to hear country music again. After watching a dozen drunken sailors and happy hookers line dancing, she wasn't ever going to try that, either. She sat in the car without turning on the ignition.

"Silence," Vik said. "Great, isn't it? It's hard to believe that anyone would sit there half the night listening to that."

As Marti watched, the lead singer and the guitar players loaded the band's equipment into a van. They had come up empty again

— nothing. Not even the few sailors the night clerk had pointed out as regulars knew anything about Liddy Fields except that she was a nice lady.

CHAPTER 7

A little before five o'clock on Tuesday morning, Marti got up. Vik had the Fields autopsy scheduled for six. The alarm was set for 6:15, which would have given her just enough time to make it in for roll call. Instead, wide awake, she was dressed and about to make coffee when Joanna came into the kitchen.

"I'm sorry," she said before Joanna could speak. "You had another softball game yesterday and I haven't made it to one yet."

Joanna rubbed at her eyes with her fist. "That's okay, Ma. You've been working too hard. Let me fix you some breakfast."

"You're hardly awake," Marti said. Joanna was not a morning person. Tendrils of auburn hair had escaped from the thick plait that hung down her back. She wore an oversized T-shirt as a nightgown, and she was barefoot.

"Sit down, Ma. Look out the window and watch what comes to the bird feeder. Theo's managed to attract some finches. And he and Mike have a great vegetable garden.

The tomatoes and squash are already a foot high."

"Squash? Your brother is growing squash?" Marti knew that was Theo's least-favorite vegetable.

"Zucchini, crookneck, and acorn."

Marti smiled. Theo would be ten in September. He seemed to do everything with enthusiasm.

"I'm paying him to grow it for me," Joanna explained. "I'm going to freeze it. We'll have great soups all winter."

Marti checked the corner of the yard reserved for the garden. The plants *were* high — plenty of growing things for plenty of healthy soups, casseroles, and salads. Having lost her father in the line of duty, Joanna remained steadfast in her efforts to keep her surviving parent healthy, primarily by attempting to control Marti's diet.

"Here," Joanna said. "Coffee, decaf."

"Where'd you get that?"

"Oh, all of it's decaf now. I just bought some and switched it with what we had. Sharon hasn't noticed, and don't you tell her."

Marti was sure that Sharon had noticed immediately and had real coffee stashed somewhere. Sharon had been Marti's best friend since grade school. Now that Marti was a widow and Sharon was divorced, they shared the upkeep on Sharon's house, and

Sharon's teaching job allowed her to be home after school with her own daughter, Lisa, and Marti's two kids.

Marti considered adding cream to the coffee, just to give it a little more flavor, then decided she still wouldn't like it. Grimacing, she blew across the surface of the cup.

"I'm sorry if I woke you," Marti said when Joanna brought the cheese and mushroom fake-egg omelette to the table. So much for real eggs, sunny-side up, and bacon and sausage. "Is everything okay with you?"

"I was going to ask you the same thing. You really have been working hard, Ma. And you look tired. You've got bags under your eyes. You should have won that volleyball tournament the Fourth of July. You're not getting any exercise."

"It's okay," Marti said. "I'm okay. I don't want you worrying about me. Vik and I know how to work smart. I'm not eating any fast foods," she lied. Frequently, that was all she had time for. "Those places serve salads, too." She got enough salads at home.

Joanna looked skeptical.

"I am, honest. I don't want you to worry."

"Watch the salad dressings," Joanna said. "Most of them are loaded with fat."

"Okay. I promise. Now go back to bed. I'm

not sure when I'll be able to get to a game, but I'll try."

"The games aren't what's important."

"I know. Some people can manage stress, Joanna. And this isn't bad stress, not for me."

Joanna gave her a hug, squeezing tightly.

"I'm fine," Marti lied. She had felt tired as hell when she got up, and now she felt guilty, too.

Marti went with Vik to see Lieutenant Dirkowitz right after roll call. The lieutenant drank decaf coffee, and two cups was more than Marti could handle in one day. She got real coffee from the machine in the basement and took it with her.

"You've got two new cases," Lieutenant Dirkowitz said.

"We know we have to postpone the vacations, sir," Vik said.

Marti knew he was being sarcastic, but he sounded cranky.

"I'm sure five homicides in three weeks seems like a vacation to MacAlister, but I'm willing to give you a couple of gofers."

"No," Vik said. "It'll be more trouble telling them what to do than doing it ourselves. Besides, they'd probably just screw up. A botched investigation is just what I don't need."

Dirkowitz looked at Marti. "How are

66

things going with the two open cases you're working on now?"

"If it weren't for a few minor details, I'd think we had a little domestic homicide with the Admunds case. As for the floater, looks like it's going to take a lot of man-hours."

The lieutenant smiled. "Something a gofer could do without screwing up?"

"Probably," Marti agreed.

Vik grunted.

"I think you two are damned close to burnout," Dirkowitz said. "Or there already, maybe. Summer's your busiest season, and it's just begun."

"We have short summers in this part of the country, sir," Vik reminded him.

"Citizens like expeditious arrests, Jessenovik, and I think they serve as a deterrent. You nailed the perp on that gang killing within twenty-four hours. Gang activity has been down a few decibels ever since. And you picked up so much peripheral information when that drug dealer went down that we've been able to cut into that activity, as well." He picked up the hand grenade he kept on his desk, a memento from his brother who had died in Vietnam. "So while I can't give you a vacation right now, I would like to free up as much of your time as possible. Someone else can do the grunt work while you concentrate on making arrests and maybe even squeeze in a little time with your families."

He smiled at Marti. "I'm glad you were able to convince Joanna to play softball for the Police League this year. We've finally got a chance for the championship. And you should have been there last night." His knuckles showed white as he squeezed the hand grenade. "You should have been there, MacAlister."

The lieutenant was coaching Joanna's team. His concern was unexpected.

"She's good, MacAlister. Very good. One kid in twenty has her eye for the ball."

Vik nudged Marti's foot with his and shifted in his chair. "Who did you have in mind to help us out, sir?"

"Who would you like?"

Marti spoke up. "Lupe Torres — if she'd take it." Two of last month's murders had occurred on Lupe's beat, and her awareness of drug and gang activity had been invaluable. "But making phone calls and canvassing aren't anything like community policing. Maybe you'd rather have her do that."

The lieutenant dropped the hand grenade, a signal that the discussion was over. "Good choice," he said. "You've got her."

"What about her partner, Burdette?" Vik asked. "I sure as hell don't want him."

The lieutenant grinned. "He'll probably

68

screw up without Torres there to keep him in line and tell him what to do. Looks like Burdette will be pulling a little traffic duty."

"There's no room for anybody else in here," Vik said as soon as he and Marti returned to their office. "It's going to take more time to keep Torres busy than to do everything ourselves."

"It might be interesting to see how she handles Slim and Cowboy."

Vik got a gleam in his eye. "Maybe we could squeeze one more desk in that corner."

"I'll organize things. It'll work. In Chicago, I was always working a case someone else had been called out on and somebody was closing a case I had opened. Seeing them through from start to finish is a luxury I never expected to have."

"This isn't Chicago."

"Vik, come on, we have evidence techs working on our cases, uniforms, all kinds of support. Now we'll have someone who does what we tell her without mouthing off."

Vik sucked his teeth, unimpressed. While Marti sorted through the morning's reports, he leaned back in his chair and threw paper clips at the wastebasket. She decided to ignore the annoying clink as metal hit metal. She and Vik were a team. He had gotten used to working with her. A male uniform might have been easier for him to accept, but Marti wanted someone she knew was reliable. She had no intentions of second-guessing or verifying someone else's work. Besides, essentially, Torres would be a clerk. She wouldn't be riding with them. It was only temporary, and Vik would have to adjust.

"Joanna has a game tomorrow," she said. "Maybe I'll be able to go."

The tap of the paper clips stopped. After a few minutes, Vik said, "So what have you got there?"

"We've dead-ended already with the Fields case. I'm giving that to Torres for a thorough background check."

"If we don't have any leads by tomorrow, let's give it to the newspaper."

"Good idea," Marti agreed. "As for the Admunds case, we haven't met the youngest daughter yet. Now's as good a time as any."

When Marti and Vik arrived at Sophia Admunds's house, Warren and Gilbert were loading some of the furniture into a rental truck parked in the driveway. A young blond woman stood near the ramp. The shorts and halter she was wearing looked like little more than a bathing suit. When she was satisfied with the way a hutch was

loaded and covered with a quilt, she gave
Warren a peck on the cheek, got into a red
Porsche parked at the curb, and drove off.

"The little woman," Vik muttered. "Interesting."

Inside, Jori and Nadya were sorting
through old correspondence.

"I don't think we should burn it," Jori
said.

"Well, it isn't worth anything." Nadya was
shorter than her sister, with softer, less
angular features, which made her look
more like her mother.

"Let's box it up, take it to the local historical society, and let them go through it,"
Jori said.

"Mother would never agree to that."

"Mother's dead, Nadya." There was a
catch in Jori's voice and everyone was silent
for a moment as she brushed at her eyes.
"Some of this dates back before the First
World War; some was grandmother's. It
seems wrong somehow to destroy it, like
saying it isn't important, that none of it
mattered."

Nadya sat back and folded her arms. "Do
what you like, Jori. You always do. But I,
for one, won't agree to it. And neither will
Warren."

"Then we just won't ask him, will we?"
Jori taped up three boxes of albums and
papers and took them into the bedroom.

71

While she was out of the room, Nadya said, "And both of you just listen to me. I'm tired of everyone picking on Warren. Ever since we were kids, he's gotten blamed for everything. Do you know how traumatizing that is for a child? To be the oldest son and always responsible for everything? No wonder . . ." She stopped for a moment and glanced at Marti and Vik. "Nobody in this family would ever do such a terrible thing as harm Mother."

Gilbert came in a few minutes later with his wife. Warren trailed behind them.

"We'll take this, too," Ellen instructed, pointing to a table.

"Ellen," Warren objected. "That's worth —"

"There are four immediate survivors, Warren," Ellen said. "You may do whatever you'd like with your fourth and everyone else's. I'm taking Gilbert's home now, before you have a chance to sell it." She followed Gilbert outside.

Nadya turned to Warren. "At least your wife isn't a little gold digger."

Jori snickered.

Warren avoided looking at or speaking to Marti or Vik. He slumped in a chair as if he was very tired.

"Better sit over here, Warren." Nadya sat, and patted the sofa cushion next to her. "I'm sure Ellen will want that chair next, if only because you're sitting on it."

Warren got up with a heavy sigh and complied.

"Now, Warren," Nadya said, patting his hand. "Since you are the executor . . ." She smiled at Jori, then turned so that her back was to her. "Why don't the four of us sit down later this evening so you can tell us what Mother would want us to do. It really isn't anyone else's business."

Vik cleared his throat and everyone looked at him. "Everything has to come back inside."

Nadya laughed.

"And, ma'am," he said to Jori, "if you want to store those boxes on the premises in a secure place, that's fine. But as you already know, nobody has cleared anything for removal."

"But —" Jori said.

"You are an officer of the court," Vik reminded her.

Nadya and Warren exchanged looks.

"Had you spoken with your mother recently?" Vik asked Nadya.

"Not since . . . I don't know, June maybe."

"Was she upset or concerned about anything when you spoke with her?"

"Mother didn't particularly like telephones. She used them only when she had to. She never called me. When I called her, she always assumed something was wrong. The last time I called, when she got over

73

her usual panic attack, she seemed fine. The only thing she complained about was her arthritis — and Warren. She always complained about Warren."

She gave her brother a sympathetic smile and pat on the arm.

"Any specific complaint?" Vik asked.

"He hadn't arranged for a neighbor boy to cut the grass."

Warren. Marti shoved the reports in the folder. Warren, executor, appraiser, real estate agent. That house. Was that what set everything in motion? "Damn it, Vik," she said.

"What?"

She took out her notes, flipped through them, checked the reports from the canvass. "Have you got anything that says anyone saw the appraiser?"

He checked. "No. Why?"

"Seven neighbors saw Warren's car on Wednesday or Friday. Nobody saw any other vehicle parked there. Nobody saw any strangers. Nobody saw the appraiser."

"Big deal."

"It probably isn't a big deal, but we both overlooked it. Damned sloppy."

His silence told her that he agreed.

There was a knock on the door and Lupe Torres, a uniformed officer, came in. Lupe looked from Vik to Marti, then shifted from one foot to the other. "Where do I sit?"

"We'll order a desk for you," Marti said.

"Kinda crowded."

"We'll manage. Vik and I are leaving in a few minutes, and you can use my desk while we're gone. There's plenty to do, most of it boring."

"That's okay." Lupe looked at Vik again.

Vik looked away.

"Pull up a chair and I'll fill you in. This is the Fields case. Body was found yesterday. Drowned — deliberately. Not your typical homicide. Not a nice way to go."

Marti brought Lupe up-to-date and explained what she needed her to do. "We're making better headway with the Admunds case. With you working on the Fields case, we might be able to close both of them."

As soon as Marti vacated her desk, Lupe got to work. Vik followed Marti out of the office. "We need to talk with Neda Wagner," he said.

"Right now," Marti agreed. "And when we get back, you'll have plenty of time to draw your time lines and diagrams and do all of the other foolishness that keeps little things like this from happening."

"It probably isn't important."

"That's not the point."

In the next two hours, they confirmed that nobody had seen the appraiser or a vehicle that could have been his. Neda Wagner couldn't pinpoint the time Sophia Admunds saw him, but Marti was able to determine that it was after Warren left, before the two women had a late lunch together at 2:00 P.M. When they stopped at Burger King and ordered Whoppers, shakes, and fries, Marti didn't feel guilty about the fat and cholesterol at all.

CHAPTER 8

Marti and Vik spent most of Wednesday attending the weekly inquests held by the coroner's office. The six jurors ruled one death accidental that Marti was certain was suicide. The jury also determined that the deaths of Sophia Admunds and Liddy Fields were homicides.

There were no family members or friends at the Fields inquest, but all of Sophia Admunds's children attended hers. Warren's wife was absent, but Ellen sat beside Gilbert, occasionally squeezing his arm.

The coroner, Janet Petroski, insisted that those presenting evidence be concise. No unnecessarily prurient details were allowed. Photographs and slides were expected to be sequential and informative, and any forensic entomologists' reports on insect activity used in determining time of death nonrepetitious. Marti would never forget the inquest for her husband, Johnny. She spent most of it with her head down and her hands covering her ears, unable to watch or listen as witness after witness and expert after expert were called to say pretty much the same thing. She found these calm and matter-of-fact presentations almost soothing in comparison, something the family members could endure without too much anguish.

When the Admunds verdict was read, Nadya hugged Warren, Ellen embraced Gilbert, and Jori sat alone, head bowed, tears coursing down her face.

By the time Marti and Vik reached their office, Lupe Torres had gone off duty. Marti scanned several pages of typed notes that Lupe had left on her desk. "Nothing new on Liddy Fields. We can't get anything out of the IRS and we haven't heard back from Social Security yet." Marti made a note to have Lupe follow up first thing in the morning.

"Lupe put together a list of Fields's newspaper clippings — the child-abuse cases by name and in chronological order and travel locations in alpha order," she told Vik.

"That sounds helpful as all hell."

"We haven't got anything much on Admunds, either. There are no indications that it was a home invasion. Nobody suspicious or unusual was observed in the neighborhood. There is nothing missing from the home. No signs of a struggle. Looks like a domestic homicide to me."

Marti flipped through the contents of her in basket. "Forensics has identified pollen on that soil sample from the Admunds house."

"Great," Vik said. "With evidence like that and all this help from Lupe, we should have both cases wrapped up before we go home tonight." He picked up his copy of Lupe's notes. "We should be doing this ourselves, MacAlister. What the hell does she know about investigating a homicide?"

"Lupe's a good cop," Marti said. "And we've got too much going on to spend time on this kind of detail."

"There's never enough time anymore. This whole damned town is going crazy."

Marti started to disagree, then realized it must seem that way to him. "Maybe it's just some kind of fluke."

"No," Vik said. "It's drugs and gangs and the general availability of firearms added to the usual greed, fear, hate, and anger." He sounded sad. "Town used to be like one big neighborhood."

"There weren't more than forty thousand people here twenty or thirty years ago. The town has . . . grown since then." She'd almost said *changed,* but Vik seemed more troubled than cranky, and that would have made him feel worse.

"So," Marti said. "What do you think? Circumstantial evidence is scarce in the Admunds case. As for Fields, let's run this sketch of the morgue shot in the newspaper."

Vik put in a call to a friend at the *News-Times*. "He'll run it tomorrow. Maybe we'll get lucky. Now," he said as he leaned back in his chair and put his hands behind his head, "we might have gotten a confession in the Admunds case by now if we'd had more time to put in on it."

"Maybe, maybe not."

"Well, they buried her Monday. Guilt should have sent one of her kids in here by now. The more time that passes after they get them in the ground . . ."

"Sometimes. It's not that predictable. We'll have financial information tomorrow. That might tell us something," Marti said. The oil on the step still bothered her. That, and the clay. She read through the forensic report. "So far, no match in Sophia's neighborhood. They're still checking out the area where Warren lives."

"And I suppose that if nothing turns up there, they'll go to Champaign. Then what? Arizona? California? And all because of half an ounce of clay."

Vik was right. One teaspoon of clay, and it would nag at them until they found why it was there and where it had come from. "I don't like these oddball loose ends, either. Now, Warren's car was observed at his mother's house when he said he was there, and she didn't die until hours later." She tapped Lupe's notes. "His secretary confirmed what he's told us about his activities on Wednesday and Friday. His wife confirms his alibi. She'll say whatever he tells her to about the times he was home." Marti thought for a minute. "If it comes to it, we could probably get his wife to contradict herself." But would they want to? Not the best kind of evidence. "It says here a neighbor also saw Warren's car parked in his driveway from seven to after midnight the night Admunds died."

"What about the appraiser?"

"Lupe hasn't been able to reach him yet. He hasn't answered any of the messages I've left."

Vik scanned Lupe's notes again. "Well, she is thorough."

"And we need this kind of help," Marti said. "Or we're going to get so bogged down in detail that we're not going to accomplish anything."

Vik's eyebrows almost met in a scowl.

"And Vik, she's a cop, not a secretary. Try to remember that, okay?"

Vik began flipping through Lupe's report in reluctant agreement.

Warren Admunds came to the precinct a little after eight Wednesday night. He slumped in the chair by Vik's desk, his head in his hands. Idly, Marti wondered if being in jail would make him less fastidious about the way he combed his hair. She pushed her chair out of his direct line of vision. Vik had had the most contact with Warren, and he had tried to establish some rapport.

"I don't want anyone else to know about this," Warren said, "but they will, won't they?" His eyes were bloodshot. It looked more like lack of sleep than too much liquor. "It just got out of hand, that's all," he said. "It just got out of hand. She wanted a house. Then she wanted a bigger house, a double lot, an in-ground swimming pool, another garage, a Cadillac convertible to put in the extra garage." He passed his hand over his head without disturbing the stripes. "It just got out of hand. I'm an economist, not a millionaire. I didn't mean to spend all of mother's money. I was going to pay it back, but when the bills started coming in, there was no way I could."

Vik waited, but Warren seemed to be talked out.

"What happened when you went to see her July third?" Vik said.

"I . . . it was awful. I knew she didn't want to move again, that she had given up as much of Grandmother's furniture as she could, that there wouldn't be any space for all of that junk she had all over the place. I knew it was important to her, but there was nothing else I could do."

"You were in a difficult position," Vik said. "You had to make some tough choices."

"Mother didn't understand that. She thought I was being selfish, thinking of myself."

"You were just doing what you had to do. You're still a young man, with a young and very attractive wife. Your life is ahead of you." Vik folded his arms. Marti could see one hand clenched in a white-knuckled fist. Warren couldn't see the fist. With luck, Warren would tell Vik what happened.

"So, Warren, how did she take it?"

"Mother . . . always got her own way . . . with Dad . . . with us. She just said she wouldn't move again and refused to say anything else."

"And then?"

"There was no arguing with her. She just pretended not to hear you. I told her the real estate agent would be coming and I left."

"Where was she when you left?"

"In the living room, with her back to me."

"What did you do while you were in the house?"

"I looked around, just to be sure there wasn't something she hadn't told me about that needed fixing."

"Where did you go?"

"To the garage, the yard, the bathroom, the . . . basement."

Vik waited a moment. "Where was your mother while you were in the basement?" he asked.

"Upstairs."

"The whole time?"

"Yes."

"Were the two of you ever near or in the basement at the same time?"

Warren shook his head. "She came to the top of the stairs, asked me what I thought I was doing, and went away when I told her. She didn't want to hear it."

"Is that what she did when she was upset? Gave you the silent treatment?"

Warren nodded.

"I really get annoyed when someone does that to me. How upset were you, Warren?"

"Pretty damned mad."

"You were in a real financial bind and she wouldn't help you at all?"

"No. And if I told her the real problem, she would have reminded me of the kind of man my father was, how he went to work every day in a factory, how he never lived beyond his means and always managed to take care of us." His voice got higher as he spoke. "How he put all of us through college and gave us the down payment on a house when we got married and left her with enough money to last the rest of her life." There was a catch in his voice. "And how selfish I was to spend all of it and how he would never forgive me for ruining her life."

"Did she say that to you, Warren?"

"Yes."

"When?"

"A few weeks ago, when I asked for a loan."

"Did she say that to you again last Wednesday?"

"No, but she would have . . . if . . ."

Vik waited. "If what?"

"If she had known. Now Gilbert and Jori will say it. Nobody understands."

"I do," Vik said. "Warren, how did your mother get to the bottom of those stairs?"

Warren put his face in his hands and began sniffling.

"What's the last thing she said to you, son?"

"That I'd never be the man my father was."

"How did you feel about that?"

"Like a stupid, incompetent fool."

"Were you angry with your mother?"

"Yes, yes I was." His voice was rising again. "She always made me mad when she said that."

"Is that why you pushed her down the stairs?"

"No, no I didn't. God knows I felt like choking her, but . . ." He stopped speaking, took a deep breath, and looked at Vik. "Is that what you think I came here to tell you? That I killed my own mother? No. She might

85

have been right — I might not be much of a man, or much of a son." He laughed quietly, then put his hand over his mouth. After a few minutes, he slumped back in the chair. "Maybe if I was a man, I would have."

Vik flexed his hand. "Warren, anybody could understand that in a situation like this, when you were under so much pressure . . ."

"I couldn't," Warren said. "Not mother. She was . . . strict. She . . . we never even talked back."

Vik looked at Warren until he looked away. "I want to believe you, sir. I know how it is when you've got a lot of responsibilities, a lot of stress."

"You don't understand." His voice quavered and he took a deep breath. "My mother died believing that I was an incompetent, ungrateful son. The last thing I said to her was, 'I can't stand you when you're unreasonable.' I didn't know that would be the last time I would see her. I didn't know that I would never speak to her again."

Vik gnawed on a corner of his lower lip. "All right, Warren. Just remember, if you need someone to talk with again, I'm here."

After Warren left, Vik led the way to the vending machines in the basement. He and Marti bought sweet rolls, potato chips, and two cans of Mellow Yellow each and went back to their office.

"If it wasn't for that oil on the step, I would have detained him," Vik said. "We've got everything: motive, method, opportunity. . . ."

"Right," Marti agreed. "But we might not have the right man."

She reached for the case folders. "We need to find out how much Sophia Admunds knew about her finances."

It was after midnight when they went home.

CHAPTER 9

Marti and Vik were called out on a drug overdose at 3:30 Thursday morning. The thirty-six-year-old woman still had the needle in her arm.

"Stupid," Vik said as Marti drove to the precinct. "Just plain stupid."

Marti yawned. Her back and shoulders ached. She was getting eight hours' sleep, but it was taking two nights instead of one.

"Court at one," Vik said. "In the meantime, there's plenty to do."

"It's about time you started delegating some of it to Lupe."

"I prefer to do some things myself, MacAlister."

"Well, I like the idea of having someone available and trained to take over some of the routine stuff. I don't have to talk with every agency in the country that can give me information about Liddy Fields. I have no compulsion to list personally each of Sophia Admunds's possessions. A summary of the assets Warren appropriated will do. It's bad enough that I've now got all these damned forms to fill out."

By the time they finished the paperwork on the drug overdose, it was time for roll call.

While Vik grouched at people over the phone, Marti drove over to talk with Neda Wagner, Sophia Admunds's neighbor. The elderly woman was kneeling under a red maple tree, weeding the begonias that circled the base of the trunk. She looked up and smiled as Marti approached.

"Back again, Detective?" Her eyes were a washed-out shade of blue and there were yellow streaks in her white hair. Standing up was a laborious process, but she waved away Marti's offer to help.

"Now," she said, dusting off her slacks at the knees, "why don't you come in and have a cup of tea."

It was cool inside. All of the shades were drawn. Everything in the kitchen was old, but not antique. The stove had legs and a warming oven and the refrigerator seemed to vibrate as it hummed. The wooden table tilted a little as Marti sat down. A ginger jar stuffed with daisies, gladioli, and snapdragons made the room seem cosy. Mrs. Wagner brewed the tea and served it with a choice of lemon or milk.

"So," Mrs. Wagner said, "Sophia did not trip and fall down the stairs or have a heart attack or something?"

"No," Marti said.

"And you do know what happened to her?"

"We think so."

The woman poured milk in her tea. "Money," she said. "It is always a bad thing when families argue about money."

"Did they argue?" Marti asked.

"No. Sophia would not argue with her children. There was a lot of her grandmother in her. I think there was some Polish nobility in her family back when. She hinted at it but never said."

"Was Sophia concerned about money?"

"No. She said there was enough, that Warren was just worried that there wouldn't be any left when she was dead. Like me, she believed her children must make their own way in the world, that she had done all that was necessary for them."

"Did she seem worried about anything lately?"

Mrs. Wagner sat very still and looked down at her hands. "I do not like to be in the middle of something that is a family matter."

"As far as I can tell, you're the only person Sophia would talk with."

"Yes, but I don't think she told me anything that can help you. Still, I suppose you should know. She did think that, with this second wife and all, Warren might be having financial problems. He had come to her for a loan, which she refused him. Sophia thought Warren wanted to get her into someplace less expensive so that she would have no need for all of her money and would not refuse to give it to him." She took a sip of tea. "She said her husband had been a smart man but that not even college could give her sons his good sense."

"Was there anything unusual about how she acted or what she said the last time you saw her?"

"She was angry because the appraiser had come, said the young gave no respect anymore. She said she called Warren and left a message on his machine that he should grow up and be a man like his father and shoulder his own responsibilities and not try to walk on her back anymore."

According to Nadya, Sophia did not like to use the phone. She must have been very upset.

"But, as far as you know, Warren did not return?"

"I didn't see his car again until Friday morning. More tea?"

Marti shook her head.

Mrs. Wagner took the teacups and pot to the sink. "Sophia was a strong woman, accustomed to having her way. But there was a sadness about her, a sorrow for something lost. I think it had something to do with her children." As she stood with her back to Marti and washed and dried the china, she said, "If you look past the trees at the back of Sophia's lot, you will see that there is a little ravine, then more trees before you come to the house on the next block. My children used to play there. They even built a playhouse once. It was like a secret place where they could hide."

Marti took a look. It would not have been difficult for Warren to park his car there and approach his mother's house without being seen.

Court took up the entire afternoon. Vik fidgeted as he waited to be called and was gruff and impatient on the stand. "They must have called seventeen sidebars," he said as they walked from the county building to the precinct. "I don't know what's wrong with people these days, shooting someone over a barking dog. It's that nuclear plant. I don't care what anyone says. It gives off something that interferes with some peoples' brain activity."

Lupe had left a copy of the News-Times on Marti's desk. Liddy Fields's picture was on the front page, with the standard headline: DO YOU KNOW THIS WOMAN? Marti put her head down, intending to rest for a minute. Vik shook her awake half an hour later. "Joanna's got a game in fifteen minutes. Think you can make it?"

Marti wondered how Vik knew that. She had forgotten.

Joanna's softball game was at a field in Gurnee, not far from an amusement park. Marti turned left just past the lot where the World War II tank was parked, then turned left again when she saw the totem pole. The game was just getting under way. Marti paused as she climbed to the top of the visitors' bleachers to watch Joanna pitch the first ball.

Leaning back, with the sun hot on her shoulders, Marti eased into the slower rhythms of the game. The first batter up was put out on a slider, the second went out with a fly ball, and the third was tagged at first base. By the third inning, the Lincoln Prairie Police League was up by two. Joanna really was into the game. She batted third, with two on base, and brought everyone in.

Marti yelled and cheered along with the dozen or so parents who had also taken the time to come. She felt so comfortable sitting on a hard bench with the hot sun toasting her shoulders and a warm breeze drying the sweat on her forehead that she didn't want the game to end. At the top of the fifth, with a six-run lead, Lieutenant

Dirkowitz sent in another pitcher. Marti went down to the dugout.

Joanna, intent on the game, yelled encouragement and instructions to the pitcher. Then she turned and saw Marti and rushed over. "Ma! This is awesome! You made it!"

"You're awesome," Marti said. "You've really improved your game this year."

Joanna grinned, reminding Marti of Momma, and cold lemonade, and all the sandlot games she had played years ago.

CHAPTER 10

When Marti reached her office Friday morning, Slim was perched on the edge of Lupe's desk.

"Why don't you go spread your charm someplace else?" Lupe said. She sounded like she meant it. Slim shifted but didn't get up. Lupe sniffed. "What is that? You take a bath in that stuff? No wonder you're trying to hit on me. Those hookers you hang with probably can't stand the smell."

Slim sauntered over to Marti and chucked her under the chin. "See? No woman can resist me."

Cowboy came in with a pitcher of water for the coffeepot. "Here you go, honey. I filled it for you."

Lupe looked around the room as if she couldn't figure out whom he was talking to.

"The coffee and the filters are right here." He opened his bottom desk drawer. "Now, you just do the best you can. It won't taste as good as mine, but as long as you're here, you might as well do something useful."

Lupe kicked her chair away as she got up, and it banged against the wall. She wasn't as tall as Cowboy, but she was broad-shouldered and broad in the hips. She walked over to the drawer, took out the can of coffee, and poured it on the floor. "I think the broom is in a closet right down the hall, honey," she said.

Slim whistled. "Ooooohwheee. And we thought Big Mac was bad. See what you get when you let two women work together? Nothing but trouble."

Cowboy kicked at the coffee grounds with the toe of his boot. "Come on, partner," he drawled. "Some folks can't even take a little joke. Looks like we might be having to find us some new quarters."

Lupe cleaned up the coffee after they left, found another can, and made a fresh pot.

"You handled that okay," Vik said.

Marti was stunned. She gave Lupe a thumbs-up.

"This coffee is about as good as Cowboy's, too. Let's get to work."

Around eleven o'clock, a uniform escorted Warren Admunds's wife into the office. Mrs. Admunds dropped a large dark blue felt bag on Marti's desk.

"One fourth of the family jewels," she said. "Paste, all of it."

Marti glanced from the bag to the woman. Mrs. Admunds was short-waisted and long-legged, with a flat rear end. Her narrow, deeply tanned face took on a waspish look as she spoke. "Oh, so that's how it is. I bring you proof that Warren had nothing whatsoever to do with his mother's death, and you're so anxious to pin it on him that you're not even interested."

"Proof, ma'am?" Marti said.

"Yes. Right here." She snatched up the bag, loosened the drawstring, and dumped out half a dozen boxes of various sizes.

"See!" She opened one and held up a necklace. Crystal and red gems caught the light and sparkled. "This is the Christmas necklace. A gift to Warren's grandmother from her second husband, Count someone or other." She snapped the case shut. "Paste, all of it. I took a bodyguard with me when I got them out of the bank vault to have them appraised." She laughed. "A bodyguard, and they're paste! Do you know what these are worth? I'm going to kill him!"

"Kill who, ma'am?"

"Gilbert. That thieving son of a bitch. He was in charge of them. He parceled them out after the will was read. Everything he gave me is paste. He's sold my jewels."

"I'm very sorry to hear that," Marti said, hoping her indifference would help maintain Mrs. Admunds's level of aggravation and keep her talking.

"Sorry? You're sorry?" For a moment, she

seemed speechless; then she took a deep breath. "Gilbert can steal from his mother's estate and it's okay, but my Warren borrows a little money and he's treated like a criminal? What kind of cop are you? Lazy? Or stupid?"

Marti decided to ignore that, at least temporarily.

"I am accustomed to getting a little more respect," Mrs. Admunds said. "Especially from those whose salaries I pay." She turned to Vik. "My husband is being harassed because he borrowed money from his mother. This is theft. Sophia's jewelry was worth quite a bit of money. And now it's gone. Gone!" She put the box back into the felt bag and pulled the drawstring. "I want you to speak with Gilbert about this at once."

"Why don't you have a seat, ma'am," Vik suggested. "Discovering something like this can be very upsetting. Maybe if I just get you a cup of coffee . . ."

Mrs. Admunds sat in the chair near Vik's desk. "Thank God someone around here understands."

"Sugar, ma'am, or sweetener?"

"Cream, if you have any, but not that powdered stuff. Otherwise, I'll take it black."

Vik brought the coffee. "Now exactly what happened to this jewelry?"

"The gems have been removed and replaced with fakes."

"All of the jewels?"

"Every one of them."

"And the settings?"

"They're real, gold and silver."

"You're sure of that?"

"Yes."

"Did anyone other than Gilbert have possession of the jewelry?"

"No. Not since his father died."

"Ma'am, do you know anything at all about Gilbert's movements on July third and fourth?"

Mrs. Admunds smiled. "Warren called him three times the afternoon of the third and he wasn't home. He called again about nine, just before he went to the store, and Gilbert still wasn't there."

According to Warren Admunds, and his neighbor, Warren hadn't left the house at all that night. No one had mentioned a trip to the store.

"Did Gilbert's wife say where he was?"

"Just that he was out."

"Did Warren try to reach him again?"

"A couple of hours later, when he got back from the store."

Two hours unaccounted for. Marti remained impassive.

"And Gilbert was still not home?"

"No, he was not."

Vik weighed the cloth bag with one hand. "May I keep a piece of the jewelry?"

"Why not? Except for what I can get for the setting, it's worthless!" She stood up and adjusted her skirt. "That lying, hypocritical thief."

"Ma'am, I'd appreciate it very much if you would give us a formal statement."

Without hesitation, Mrs. Admunds agreed.

When Vik came back, he was rubbing his hands together. "We've got everything," he said. "The telephone calls, the two-hour trip to the store, everything. Neither Gilbert nor Warren has an alibi." He threw the Styrofoam cup of coffee he had given Mrs. Admunds into the wastebasket. "Greed. With all that she has, she's so angry because she won't have more, she doesn't even realize she's given us almost enough to put her husband in jail — unless, of course, Gilbert did it."

"Does this mean another trip to Champaign?"

"Sounds like a good idea to me."

"Not today, right? It's —" She checked her watch. "We'll hit rush-hour traffic."

"If we leave right away, we might get there before Gilbert gets wind of this."

It was almost eight o'clock when they arrived at Gilbert's rambling wood-frame house.

"I wonder why he'd sell his mother's crown jewels," Vik said as they negotiated the toy-strewn walk. "His wife inherited this place. He's got tenure at the University of Illinois." He kicked at a big yellow dump truck. "Probably something simple and straightforward — like greed, sloth, envy, or all of the above."

They could hear the children before they reached the front porch. The baby was screaming, and two of the boys were fighting over what they were going to watch on TV.

As Ellen Admunds opened the door, she called over her shoulder, "Stop hitting your brother and sit down, all of you, right now!"

"Ma'am?"

She took a step back and said, "Oh, it's you again. *Now* what do you want?" The smallest boy came up behind her and wrapped his arms around her legs.

"Gilbert should be here any minute now," she said. She turned around and shouted, "Your daddy will be here in about five minutes. You'd better get those toys picked up. Now!"

The oldest boy ran toward them, then reached for his brother as he veered away, knocking him to the floor. He made a face, then ran up the stairs.

"I'm gonna tell Daddy!" the younger boy called as he got up.

"Are you all right?" Ellen asked.

Screwing up his face, the boy began to cry. Before his mother could comfort him, the baby began to cry, too.

In the time it took Marti to follow the woman to the living room, the baby's screams reached decibels she hadn't heard in years.

The room had been a mess when they were there on Saturday. Today, it was worse. Clothes were strewn about and toys littered the floor. A soiled diaper hadn't been disposed of, and someone had spilled orange Jell-O on the green carpet.

Ellen sat down, put the baby across her knees, and began jiggling her legs. "My au pair got homesick and went back to England," she explained. The baby put her thumb in her mouth and made loud sucking noises. "I don't know what I'm going to do until Gilbert finds a replacement."

Vik raised his eyebrows just enough to let Marti know he considered having an au pair somewhat unusual. Marti looked toward the ceiling, then glanced around the room. She wondered how they could afford the help, but everything was so out of control that it was probably more of a necessity than an extravagance.

Upstairs, the boys shrieked. Ellen ignored them, as well as the thumping overhead.

"Thank God," Ellen said. "They're in the

102

attic. They have a playroom up there."

Marti decided against asking if it was safe to leave them alone.

"It looks like Gilbert is going to be late. Sometimes when he gets to talking with his students, he loses all track of time."

After a few minutes, when the baby was asleep, Vik took a jewelry case out of his pocket.

Ellen looked surprised. "Why do you have Mother Admunds's jewelry?"

He opened the case, displaying the Christmas necklace.

"Beautiful, isn't it?" Ellen said. "I would have loved to have it, but Mother Admunds said it was for Warren."

"Warren," Vik asked, "or his wife?"

"Warren. Mother Admunds didn't want any of it to leave the immediate family. We can wear it, but it belongs to our husbands. It's in her will."

"And you have some of her jewelry, too?"

"Oh yes, some lovely pieces."

Upstairs, a child yelled, "Stop it!" then began to cry.

Gilbert came home a few minutes later. When Vik showed him the Christmas necklace, he turned so pale, Marti thought he was going to pass out. Before either man could say anything, the three boys came running downstairs and chaos reigned again. Vik looked at Marti and shook his

103

head. He took Gilbert to one side and spoke softly, jabbing his finger for emphasis. As Vik spoke, the smallest boy went up to him and punched him in the thigh.

Vik held the child by the arm and squatted beside him.

"Young man, do you know that I'm a police officer?"

The child gave him a surly look and shook his head.

"Have you ever heard of disturbing the peace?"

Another shake of the head.

"That's what all of this screaming and fighting and hitting is. It's against the law. People go to jail for behaving like this."

The boy's lower lip jutted out.

"This is not acceptable behavior. Do you understand that?"

The boy gave a slight, reluctant nod.

"I can't hear you nod your head," Vik said. "You have to say, 'Yes, sir.' Then I know you understand."

"Yes, sir." The boy didn't look at Vik as he spoke.

Vik let go of his arm.

"Remember," Vik said, "disturbing the peace."

"Yes, sir."

"Look at me." Vik tousled the boy's dark hair and smiled.

Still shaken, Gilbert said nothing. Ellen

glared at Vik as if he'd just committed child abuse. Marti recalled what Warren had said about his mother being strict. If that was true, Sophia Admunds must have found the permissiveness in this house intolerable.

While Ellen took the boys upstairs to get ready for bed, Marti and Vik joined Gilbert in the living room. Gilbert rubbed the stubble of beard that darkened his jaw. He looked at Vik. "I can't believe how quickly you found out about the jewelry."

Vik put the Christmas necklace on the table. "This must have given your mother a great deal of pleasure."

"She never wore it," he said. "Nobody ever wore it. The jewelry was too valuable to be worn. It was kept in the safe-deposit box. And the money I got for the gems isn't gone." He swallowed hard. "This should have been sold years ago, when Dad was sick and they needed the money to keep Grandmother's house. That's why I did it, so Mother wouldn't have to leave her home again. For once, Warren could stand and watch while I took care of everything."

There was a catch in his voice and he looked down at his hands. "The one time I did something right, after Warren screwed things up, and she died without even knowing."

As they walked to the car, Vik said, "Hard to imagine two adults having absolutely no control over four children who are all under the age of seven and less than four and half feet tall." Plastic cracked as he stepped on the toys that littered the walk.

Ben was watching a movie in the den when Marti got home.

"Please don't say I look tired."

"Hungry?" he asked instead.

"No. Where are the kids?"

"In bed. It's almost midnight."

"Oh." Marti collapsed in the recliner and kicked off her shoes. "Joanna, too?"

"Uh-huh. She's really into her game. Even her boyfriend is playing second fiddle to softball."

"Smart girl." Marti closed her eyes. "Is everyone okay?"

"They're fine. And you made it to Joanna's game last night. I was on duty."

"Vik reminded me," Marti admitted. "I've lost track of everything — her schedule, your schedule. And I really want to watch her play. She's at the top of her game."

"I've got most of them on video. But don't let her know I told you. It's a surprise."

Without opening her eyes, Marti took Ben's hand and squeezed it. "Thanks. You don't make me feel guilty."

"This is what you do, Marti. And you're damned good at it. None of us can imagine you doing anything else. And it isn't just that we need to see you. You need to see us, too." Ben brushed a few strands of hair from her forehead. "We'll work it out. Want anything before I go?"

"A kiss, maybe. And a beer."

Ben shook her awake before he left. She went upstairs and fell across the bed fully clothed.

CHAPTER 11

Marti slept in Saturday morning. When she got to the precinct, Slim was working his way through everything in his in basket, Cowboy was fixing a pot of coffee, and Vik had a rather smug expression on his face. Lupe was typing.

"Anything new?" Marti asked.

"Two calls on the Fields photo," Lupe said. "Look in your in basket."

The room was too quiet. Marti caught Vik's eye and shrugged. Vik shook his head. From the way his lips were compressed, Marti could tell he was suppressing a snicker.

"You working on the Admunds case?"

He nodded.

"Have you confirmed that Gilbert still has the money from the sale of the family jewels?"

He gave another nod. His mouth looked like he had just swallowed lemon juice. Marti decided to stop trying to make him laugh.

She reached for Liddy's file. "I'll keep working on Fields." Nobody spoke as Marti added to her notes.

Slim and Cowboy left without saying a word. She wondered what had happened before she got there. When she went through her incoming mail, she found a copy of Fields's employment history from Social Security. Liddy had worked at the motel for two years. Prior to that, she'd had several jobs managing apartment buildings in Lincoln Prairie. The pension from the state of Rhode Island was for working in a facility for the mentally retarded for fifteen years. Between that job and managing buildings, she had worked in three states as a teacher's aide, including nine years in Nashville at a state school for girls. Most recently, she had worked at two schools in Lincoln Prairie.

Marti split the employment list with Lupe, taking the most recent herself. By noon, Marti had a contact person for each job on her list. A half hour later, she had found only one person at home, the former principal at Central Elementary, the last school where Fields had worked. He repeated Liddy's name several times before he said, "Oh, yes, her" in a disapproving tone. "She thought she was the school social worker. An interfering busybody who thought she knew all there was to know about raising and educating children. An interesting notion, since she never had one of her own.

The district was well rid of her."

"Did she leave voluntarily?"

"Yes. She did her job and she was very good with the children. She was just too opinionated. We were all relieved when she resigned."

"What reason did she give?"

He thought for a minute. "Something vague — disillusionment with the way the system dealt with children. As if she even had the education to understand a concept like that."

"Did you hire her?"

"Yes, but she had excellent references, and as I said, she was very effective with the children. It was . . . everything else. I don't think the woman had one opinion, erroneous or accurate, that she kept to herself. And most were erroneous."

Resisting the impulse to ask by whose assessment, Marti got the names of two teachers Liddy had worked with, then thanked him.

"Nothing about this case is easy," she said half an hour later. The teachers had retired and moved out of town.

She tried the two women who had called the precinct. The first, Inez Santiago, had taught at Central Elementary and was also retired. Marti wondered, since the principal hadn't mentioned her, if Santiago was someone who liked Liddy Fields. Perhaps she was even a friend.

"Let's go, Jessenovik. Santiago lives in that senior citizens' high-rise on Garfield."

"Great." Vik stood up and stretched. "A senior citizen, huh? Sounds like you might have a live one. How old do you think she is — eighty-five?"

Lupe giggled and got the full effect of Vik's scowl.

"What happened before I came in this morning?" Marti asked Vik as soon as Lupe was out of earshot.

"I'm not sure. Cowboy wanted Lupe to make some Mexican pastry or cookie or something. She ignored him. Cowboy said something in Spanish. Lupe said something in Spanish that Cowboy didn't understand. Slim said, 'I wouldn't let her talk about my mother like that,' but he refused to translate. Lupe said they were both sexist SOBs and made a few comments about their manhood when they refused an invitation to take care of it in the parking lot. Then everyone shut up."

"What did you do while all of this was going on?"

"Nothing. Lupe can handle herself — same as you. She just can't put them down with a look the way you can. She gets more aggressive."

"Assertive," Marti corrected.

"Whatever."

Inez Santiago lived on the sixth floor of the high-rise. She was a tiny woman with intense dark eyes that seemed to sparkle. Her hips swayed as she led them to a small balcony. She walked like a young girl.

"I saw the picture and the story about Liddy in the newspaper. I called, but I have nothing to tell."

The balcony was on the east side of the building. It was almost two o'clock. They were sitting in the shade, but it was hot. A slight breeze off the lake had died down, and as Marti listened to the old woman, the heat settled about her like a blanket.

"But you knew her."

"Yes, I knew her. We all knew her. We did not invite her to our homes or ask her to go with us when we went to a play. She did not attend those parties we held at school. She worked very well with the children — even the most difficult. She would wear the worst of them down with her kindness until they could not continue to be rude."

"But you didn't socialize with her," Marti said.

"Because we did not feel that she liked us, that she approved of the ways we taught children. She was very courteous with them, very critical of us."

"Do you know why she stopped working with children?"

Inez Santiago looked in the direction of the lake. In profile, there was a sternness about her that implied rigidity.

"She became sad that last year. She was quiet. She stopped complaining, but she also stopped . . . giving. It was as if something in her spirit was gone, as if somehow she wasn't there with us any-more."

"You don't know what happened?"

"No. We never asked. She never said."

Marti signaled Vik. Time to go. This was going nowhere. "Was there anyone she seemed to be friends with? Anyone she might have talked to?"

"Not that I can think of. The school social worker, maybe. She came in a couple of times a week. Or the nurse. I think she works at Lincoln Prairie General now."

Back in the car, Marti said, "The other woman who called was the school nurse. I'll bet that principal didn't give us the name of anyone who might be helpful. I'm going to see her next, at the hospital."

"I'm sure she'll know at least as much as Santiago. Not a hell of a lot. Drop me off at the precinct," Vik said.

"You just don't like hospitals."

"Don't drag this out, Marti. Either the woman has something to tell you or she doesn't. Fields might have been the chatty type, but she doesn't seem to have been

113

Miss Popularity. Doesn't Joanna have a game today?"

"I don't think so. If she does, she'll understand if I'm not there. If we don't get something on this Fields case pretty soon, whatever sources we might have will dry up."

"I'm not sure there are any sources. None that are worth anything, anyway."

"Neither am I," Marti admitted.

By the time Marti walked from the parking lot to Lincoln Prairie General's main entrance, she was perspiring. That morning, the weather report said that the temperatures would meet or exceed yesterday's high of 98°, with a heat index of 115. Marti thought both predictions were a bit low. The lobby was cool, and as she headed for the information desk, a tall woman wearing a navy blue smock over white slacks came toward her.

"Detective MacAlister? I'm Gwen Pelham."

Up close, her hair was more gray than blond, and there were deep creases at the corners of her eyes, which were a deep, clear blue. She lead the way to several chairs grouped around an arrangement of plants. Marti chose a chair away from the windows and the glare of the sun.

"It's been a long time since I worked for the school district," Pelham said. "I saw

Liddy's picture in the paper, but I haven't spoken with her in years."

"We haven't been able to locate any next of kin," Marti said. The chairs were comfortable enough to take a nap in. They were nothing like those in the waiting rooms.

Pelham hesitated. "She spoke of a daughter occasionally, but in the past tense, as if she wasn't around anymore. And when she did, it was almost as if it was a slip of the tongue, something she didn't mean to talk about. She always swore me to secrecy, so I never told anyone. I never asked any questions, either. She was always so good with the children, just loved them. If she did have one of her own and the child is still living, I can't imagine her daughter not keeping in touch."

"Did she mention a name?"

"No. At one point, I thought she might have had a miscarriage, or even an abortion. Then she said something about being in Memphis or Nashville and wishing that they lived near the ocean so she could teach her to swim. Loved water, Liddy did. Strange, the way she died."

When Marti reached the precinct, Vik was working at his desk and Lupe at hers.

"The appraiser called," Vik said. "He had the Admunds appraisal scheduled for Monday and has no idea why we thought he

115

might have been there July third. He had already left town."

"But Sophia told Neda he was there. If he wasn't, who was?"

"I don't know, MacAlister, but there's nothing to indicate that Admunds was senile, so my guess is that someone was there."

"Damn," Marti said. Another loose end.

"Where's the Testosterone Twosome?" Marti asked.

"I suggested that they might try corralling a toothless eighty-seven-year-old hooker who gives good head," Lupe said.

Vik came close to smiling.

Marti pulled Fields's autopsy report. "Fields had a hysterectomy."

"And?"

"She could have had a child before that."

"Did you find out something about next of kin?"

"Just that there might be a daughter." She checked the employment record. "While she was living in Nashville. She stayed there nine years."

Lupe rolled a sheet of paper out of the typewriter. "I'm not sure what I've got, but it might be something. I contacted someone in Rhode Island who worked in the same residential facility as Fields at about the same time. He didn't remember Fields, but he said a child wandered away during the winter and was found dead in the woods that spring. I called their local newspaper and library and they're going to fax whatever they've got on it."

Marti scanned Lupe's notes. "Good work."

"It happened twenty years ago."

"But it happened about the time she left. She lived in three states before settling here, and she left another job that involved children."

"Big deal," Vik said.

"Maybe there's some kind of pattern."

"And when we figure out just what that pattern is, MacAlister, is it going to tell us who killed her?"

"Look, we're finally beginning to get some information, so who knows."

"Let me know when you have something that might get us somewhere."

Marti wadded up a piece of paper and threw it at him. "Check out Sophia Admunds's financial records. Let me know when you find something meaningful there."

She told Lupe to find out whatever she could about Liddy's nine years in Nashville.

"Kids," Vik said.

"Huh?"

"None of the adults saw anyone at Admunds's house on the third, but there are

117

kids in the neighborhood."

"Uniforms talked with the kids."

"We didn't."

"Right," Marti said. "Here we go again."

They came up empty and were ready to go home when the sergeant called from the front desk. An Alma and Darred Miller wanted to see them.

"Now what?" Vik said. "I never heard of them."

When Marti looked at Alma Miller, the first word that came to mind was *ordinary*. Alma was short and plump, with plain brown hair. Then Marti looked into her eyes, deep brown wells filled with sadness. It was as if she had seen every sad thing that had ever happened.

Darred, a tall scarecrow of a man, handed Marti a newspaper clipping of the artist's sketch of Liddy Fields.

"You knew her?" Marti said.

"No," the man said. "But Alma here, she knows that someone held that woman under the water until she drowned."

"How do you know that, ma'am?" Marti asked.

"I dreamed it."

Marti heard a sharp intake of breath. Vik was not pleased.

"When did you dream it, ma'am?"

"Sunday night."

"She woke up at eleven-fifty-three," her husband said.

"How did you know it was Liddy Fields in your dream?" Marti asked.

"Oh, I didn't. Not until I saw this in the newspaper. Sometimes I never know who it is."

Vik came over. "You've had other dreams?"

"Oh, yes, most of my life."

"Bad dreams?" Vik said.

The woman looked down at her hands. "Most often, yes."

"When's the last time you had one of these dreams?" Vik asked. "Before this one, I mean."

"Oh, I don't know, maybe a year ago."

"In March," her husband said. "I never did see anything in the newspaper that could have been what she dreamed about."

Vik scratched his head. "And what precipitates these dreams, ma'am? What causes them? Is it something you eat?"

Alma seemed puzzled. "I'm afraid I don't know. They just come."

"And where do you live, ma'am?" When she replied, Vik wrote the address down. "We really appreciate your coming in like this, and so late at night."

Marti hoped they missed the sarcasm. It was only a little after eight.

"We just got back from our trailer in

Wisconsin," her husband said. "We came right away."

"And we do appreciate it when public-spirited citizens such as yourself come in and . . . provide information," Vik said, then ushered them to the door.

"Wait," Marti said. "What else do you know about Liddy Fields?"

Vik's eyebrows met above the bridge of his nose.

"Just that she was one with the water, she loved to swim, and there was a burden in her heart."

Vik walked them out and returned a few minutes later with two cans of cola.

"We're out of Mello Yello," he said.

"If you don't stop frowning like that, Jessenovik, your eyebrows are going to bunch up permanently."

"You didn't have to encourage her."

"Encourage her? Hell, I believed her," Marti said.

"I sort of got that impression, and I'm sure she did, too. Another crackpot for your collection. Now we'll get phone calls from our friendly local psychic every day, and you are going to take every one of them."

Marti had grown up knowing half a dozen women who could "see." Miss Lucy could tell you if you were pregnant before you missed a period. Miss Dolly knew if you had sickness and approximately where it was.

Aunt Rosetta Grey knew when death was coming. And, like Alma Miller, Mother Henderson had dreams.

Vik waved a piece of paper in front of Marti. "Do you see where they live?"

She read the address. "So?"

"Four blocks from the nuclear plant. What did I tell you?"

"Oh come on, Jessenovik, you don't believe that."

"Well, it has to be something." He drained his can of cola. "Two cases in a week, and now this, some well-intentioned, addle-brained airhead who has dreams. Fields's picture is in the newspaper for one day and already it's attracting all the weirdos."

CHAPTER 12

Marti looked out the office window for about half an hour after the Millers left. There wasn't much of a view, but the sky was dark and clear above the roof-tops and tree branches and she could see a few stars. Stars. Liddy Fields. Marti didn't consider herself superstitious, but she did believe there were things some people could discern that others could not. She couldn't just disregard Alma's dream. The day Liddy was found floating in the swimming pool, there had been a plane crash on the East Coast and a record number of heat-related deaths in the Midwest. The newspaper coverage of her death had been confined to a column entitled the "Police Blotter" in the *News-Times*. Liddy's death had been reported in two sentences.

Marti pulled that clipping from her file. "The manager of the Ship's Out Motel was found dead in the cabana by an out-of-state visitor taking an early-morning swim. There are no further details, pending an autopsy." The autopsy didn't make the newspaper. There was nothing else until they published that sketch.

How did Alma Miller know that Liddy Fields had been held underwater? How did she know that Fields had drowned? How did she know she had loved water? And what was the sadness of heart that Alma referred to?

"MacAlister," Vik said, "you're letting this nutcase get to you. And don't give me that instinct crap. You know and I know that some cases just draw them out of the woodwork. I'm surprised this Miller woman is the only one."

Marti started to point out what Alma Miller knew, then changed her mind. Vik would just insist there was some logical explanation. Maybe there was. She began going through Liddy's file again, page by page.

"It's getting late," Vik said.

Marti gestured toward the slim stack of papers. "There's no next of kin listed anywhere. Nobody has claimed Fields's body. Nobody has so much as inquired about a funeral."

Vik ran his fingers through his hair. "Okay," he said. "One more time."

They began going through Lupe's summaries of Liddy's newspaper clippings. Most were cases that had received national attention. In all but two, there had been an arrest and a conviction.

"Here's one on Natalie Beatty," Vik said.

"I remember that one."

It was one of the unsolved cases, and the only one that happened in Illinois. "Seven years and they've never found her?" Marti said.

Vik shook his head.

"Did you work on the case?"

"No. It happened in McHenry, but they lived here before moving there. Not too far from Garden Place."

"Where Admunds used to live." Marti scanned the article, checked her notes and a few dates. "All of these cases have something to do with abused or missing children. I wonder why."

"We'll never know," Vik said. He stood up and stretched. "I know the perps aren't getting any smarter, so I must be getting old." He yawned. "I can't remember the last time I had a case with a teaspoon of clay and two grains of pollen as the primary evidence and another with newspaper clippings from fifteen states that go back twenty years." He yawned.

Marti's eyes were beginning to burn. "We're both overtired," she said.

Tomorrow she would call everyone she had spoken to about Liddy. There had to be more leads. If a stranger could come in and tell her how Liddy died, there had to be someone, somewhere, who had some clue about why.

It was a few minutes past eleven when she got home. She found a note propped against Joanna's softball glove on the kitchen table. Sharon had gone out to dinner with the current Mr. Wonderful, Theo was with Ben and Mike, Lisa was staying at a friend's house, and Joanna was upstairs. Marti picked up the glove. When Johnny gave it to Joanna for her ninth birthday, it was too big. Now the leather was soft and worn and fit just right.

Marti took the glove upstairs with her. Joanna was curled up on her side, sound asleep. In the dim light from the hall, she looked younger than fifteen. Marti could see herself and her mother in the soft, full contours of Joanna's face. She should have gone to her game tonight. How could she not do her job? Perspective, priorities — she was losing all sense of that. Maybe tomorrow they could go jogging in the forest preserve.

Marti returned to the kitchen and sat in the rocker. In the moonlight, she could see Theo's garden. The badminton set was set up between two trees. Someone had left the cover open on the grill and pop cans on the picnic table. Her stomach tumbled. She had worked through the evening without taking time for supper and had gotten nowhere. She didn't understand her compulsion to solve the Fields case. As Vik said, it wasn't the crime of the century. And as far as she had determined, there wasn't anyone out there who cared.

If Liddy Fields had any family of record, the government agencies she had contacted would have had to notify them before releasing information. But even if there was no next of kin, how had Liddy Fields managed to live sixty-six years without making any friends? Were there friends somewhere in her past who had lost touch? Or had everyone kept their distance, like Inez Santiago? A nice lady, the clerk at the motel had said, but he didn't know anything about her, either.

It would seem that Fields had had a way with children, but for some reason she had turned away from them. Maybe Liddy Fields had been too busy to make friends.

Marti was dozing off in the chair when Sharon came in. Without opening her eyes, Marti followed the sound of Sharon's movements. High heels tapped against the tile floor, followed by two thuds as Sharon took off her shoes and tossed them into the corner.

"You're early. It's not even midnight," Marti said.

"If Mr. Wonderful hadn't pestered me all week, I would have stayed home. And I sure should have. I sure won't be seeing him again." The beads woven into Sharon's dozens of braids clicked as she walked to the refrigerator. "You're home early, too. Ben should be back with the boys soon." She grinned. "After the kids are all asleep, you two could tiptoe on upstairs, or go over to his place and have a good time. Nobody would know but me. And I wouldn't tell."

"I don't think so."

"Marti, I know you've been busy and we haven't had much chance to talk, but don't tell me you two ain't doing the dirty yet?"

Marti closed her eyes and smiled.

"Look, Marti, I know you don't expect this man to love 'pure and chaste from afar' forever. This must be more serious than I thought. There's no other way to explain why he's been hanging around this long."

"We're . . . courting," Marti said.

"Courting? Girl, you are out of your mind. This is almost the twenty-first century, not the nineteenth. Now I know things were different when you and Johnny were dating. Your momma was right there and you spent most of your time in church, but things don't work that way no more."

"Maybe not," Marti agreed.

"Men expect you to put out. And there're plenty of women out there willing to if you're not."

"I suppose so."

"And you don't care?"

"Maybe I'm just out of touch," Marti admitted.

"Maybe you just want too much."

"You think so?" Marti said. What did she want?

"What if you can't have it all? What if you hold out for something that isn't there? Are you willing to settle for nothing?"

"Maybe." She would rather do that than settle for something she didn't want.

"Marti, you're almost forty years old, and you've got two kids. You've got to be realistic. As men go, Ben's not bad. I'd hang on to him if I were you. He's steady, reliable. You and Johnny, that was one thing. I sat in the same room with you two and watched that man make love to you with his eyes. Something like that doesn't come along more than once. Don't hold out for the magic. You had it already."

Marti wasn't sure how she felt about what Sharon called magic. She wasn't even sure what that was. Things had just felt right with Johnny. She thought everything felt right with Ben, too. She just wanted to be sure. Her stomach tumbled as she watched Sharon rummaging through the refrigerator.

"Marti, sometimes when you haven't been with but one man, you need the experience. You just need to do it, sleep with someone. It doesn't have to be love and it doesn't have to be forever. It's just something to get the old hormones stirring again."

"I haven't had time to sort all of that out," Marti said. "And I'm not sure I agree. I don't want just any old warm body." She didn't want any one-night stands, either. After Johnny, that could never be enough.

"What do you want?"

She didn't want someone who was too much like Johnny. She'd make comparisons forever and never be happy. "Something different. Something I haven't had before. Something new." And something permanent, something she could rely on. Was she expecting too much?

Sharon put the kettle on for tea. "You'd better settle for Ben or you'll be waiting a long time, maybe forever. Hungry?"

"It's about time you asked. Have we got anything easy?"

"Joanna made a pretty decent chicken salad tonight. It's got Granny Smith apples and pineapple and honeydew melon in it, and some kind of dressing with honey and crushed walnuts."

"Sounds . . . healthy."

Sharon laughed.

Ben came in with the boys just after midnight.

"We went fishing in the dark," Theo said. "We didn't catch anything, but it was real scary sitting in the boat with the frogs and the crickets, and we heard an owl."

Marti gave him a hug. "We saw a skunk, too. And a raccoon that was a lot bigger than the ones we see around here. Know what? I'm going to put up a bat house in the yard. That would be neat, having a bat living here. He'd eat all of the insects."

Ben hustled the boys upstairs and put them to bed.

"You working tonight?" Marti asked when he came down.

"No. I've got tonight and tomorrow night off. What's up with you?"

She shook her head. "I missed Joanna's game today and she was asleep when I got home, so I didn't get to say I was sorry."

"The boys and I were there. As far as I can tell, the kids are okay. Not spending time with them is bothering you."

"I've dealt with enough kids who nobody had time for."

"But Sharon has time for them, I have time for them, and you do the best you can. They understand that. I think you need to spend time with them for yourself. You're the one missing out."

Marti thought about that for a minute and decided he was right.

"So, let's work on it from that angle," Ben said.

"How?"

"I don't know. Let me think about it."

Before he left, he fixed her a cup of chamomile tea.

"Sharon thinks I should grab you," she said. "Quick."

"Oh? That's not such a bad idea."

"She thinks I'm holding out for something that isn't going to happen."

"What?"

"Magic."

"Do you agree?"

She looked down at the tea, which was fixed exactly the way she liked it, thought of the boys falling asleep upstairs and dreaming of night sounds and night creatures. She thought of Joanna looking up and seeing someone who cared about her cheering from the stands. "I don't think Sharon knows what magic is." Marti went to him, felt his arms strong around her and his lips firm against hers. Sharon didn't understand magic at all.

CHAPTER 13

Marti attended the adult Bible study group with Ben while the kids were in Sunday school, but she left before morning services began. When she got to the precinct, there was a message from Vik that he would be in after Mass. She hummed as she made a pot of coffee she hoped was diluted enough so that nobody would complain. Then she got on the telephone.

"Mildred made some bubble bread," Vik said when he came in. The aroma of honey and walnuts and cinnamon wafted up as he unwrapped it. "Have you contacted anyone with information about Fields yet?"

The telephone rang as Marti was about to say no. The caller identified herself as Tyree Laws.

"I've been trying to get through to you for over an hour. You're the detective assigned to the Fields case?"

"You knew Liddy Fields?" Marti said. Vik gave her a thumbs-down, cautioning against optimism.

"My sister and I used to live in Lincoln Prairie. We're in Racine now, but we still attend Saint John's Episcopal on Pine. We heard about Liddy this morning and thought we should call. We worked with her at Park Elementary."

Marti got the woman's address.

"She didn't say anything about a crystal ball, did she?" Vik asked when Marti hung up. "If I see a Ouija board or tarot cards at her house, I'm leaving." He got his cup, reached for the spigot on the coffeepot, then hesitated. "Did you make this, MacAlister? It doesn't smell like Cowboy's."

"Slim and Cowboy didn't come in this morning. I hope it's not some kind of protest."

"Maybe they're boycotting because they can't handle two females in the same office. They're behaving like idiots."

Marti was speechless. This from a man who didn't think women belonged on the force when she came here three years ago.

"What do you know," Vik said. "I can stir this with a spoon." He tasted it.

"Anything else on the Fields-Nashville connection?"

"I'm going to have Lupe get that sketch of the morgue shot in as many Tennessee newspapers as possible."

They left some bubble bread next to the coffeepot in case Slim and Cowboy came in and then they headed for Racine.

Tyree Laws lived in a small brick bungalow identical to the other brick bungalows on a block-long dead-end street. The only thing that set her house apart from the others was the ramp beside the front steps. When Laws opened the door, she was in a wheelchair. She was plump and brown-skinned with a scattering of tiny black moles on her face. Gray-streaked hair was pulled away from her face and fastened in a French twist. Marti looked at Laws's hands and decided she was nearing sixty, although she looked closer to fifty.

"Oh dear," Laws said as they showed her their shields. "It's hard to believe you're here because of Liddy. She was the last person in the world you'd ever expect to have anything to do with the police."

They followed her through the living room and into a kitchen, where the counters were scaled to her height in the wheelchair.

"How well did you know Liddy Fields?" Marti asked.

"Probably better than most people. She didn't make friends easily. Liddy was the teacher's aide for kindergarten through grade three. Tyrell, my sister, taught first grade, so she saw more of her than I did. I taught fourth."

"We haven't been able to locate any next of kin."

"Liddy's mother died when she was ten. She lived in foster homes until she was sixteen. Then she just kind of drifted."

"She told you that?"

"Yes. . . . Oh, Stan." A cat, striped in shades of gray, stood in the doorway. With a soft purr, it jumped up and settled on Tyree's lap.

"Did she ever talk about living in Nashville?"

"Just that it was too far from the ocean."

"That's it?"

"Liddy talked a lot without saying much of anything. She didn't trust many people. I think that was her way of keeping them away."

"Children seem to have been important to her," Marti said.

"She had difficulty relating to the older ones. She dressed funny, 'shabby chic' I called it, and she talked a lot about the good old days. I think she made up most of that. The fourth and fifth graders made fun of her. She was wonderful with the younger children, though."

Tyree rubbed the cat between the ears. It closed its eyes and purred. "We had this new boy one year who was horrid — eight years old, and he cussed, sneaked his father's cigarettes, and gave impromptu antienvironmental speeches in class. His third day in school, he ran into Liddy — literally. Knocked her down. And she got hold of him and didn't turn him loose until he was on the honor roll."

A door closed. "Tyree," a woman's voice called.

"In the kitchen."

A moment later, a woman who must have been Tyree's twin came into the room. She put two plastic grocery bags on the counter. "You must be police officers. What happened to Liddy?"

"Have you kept in touch with her?" Marti asked.

"Liddy wasn't much for that kind of thing. We did exchange Christmas cards." She put eggs and bread in the refrigerator and looked over her shoulder. "Nobody seems to be saying what happened."

"We're not sure," Marti said. Vik had not been able to determine how Alma Miller knew as much as she did. Marti agreed that no further information about the case should be divulged. "What can you tell me about her?"

Tyrell pulled up a chair near her sister. "Liddy understood children in a way that a lot of us did not — little things. We would collect warm clothing when it got cold and send children to the nurse when we saw that they needed something."

Tyree interjected, "Liddy was so critical of everything that people tended not to hear what she was saying. When she told us the children were embarrassed by our charity, everyone was offended. But when Tyrell and I asked those children to stay after and help in class like Liddy suggested, and quietly saw that they got what they needed . . ."

"The children tended to lose the clothing we gave them," Tyrell said. "But when we began giving things to them less conspicuously, they wore them all winter."

"Not that many of the other teachers would listen," Tyree said. The cat resettled itself on her lap, blinked, and purred louder.

"Because it was Liddy's idea," Tyrell said.

"Then having that little Natalie Beatty go missing after Liddy had been insisting for so long that something was wrong . . ."

"Lord," Tyrell said. "And to think she almost got fired over that."

"Fired?" Marti said.

"She knew that little girl was being abused," Tyree said.

"None of the rest of us believed her. She was such a well-behaved, well-mannered, well-dressed little girl. Her parents seemed like such nice people."

"Her mother," Tyree said. "We never did meet the father. Having little Natalie go missing took a lot out of everyone. Tyree and I took early retirement. As soon as we could, we moved here." Marti glanced at Vik and remembered the clipping among Fields's papers. He knew much more about the Beatty case than she did. Did they want to pursue this? She turned her hand palm up, but he didn't take over. "And Liddy Fields knew Natalie?"

"We all knew Natalie. From kindergarten. She was going into third grade when she disappeared, but we all knew her. She was just the cutest little thing — small for her age, with long dark hair and the prettiest big brown eyes. And she wore the cutest dresses. She looked like a little doll. Quiet, though. Timid. Ate like a bird. Sickly, her mother said, but she wasn't absent a lot."

Marti was at a loss for what to say next. She frowned at Vik. "Natalie attended Park Elementary?"

"Yes. In Lincoln Prairie," Tyree explained. "She started in kindergarten. When Liddy reported the abuse, Natalie was in second grade. DCFS took Natalie and her two brothers right after school was out for the summer, and Liddy didn't come back — she transferred to Central. Natalie and the boys were returned to their parents the following summer and Natalie went missing. Liddy stayed at Central for a year after Natalie disappeared; then she quit. Said she couldn't stand to see what kept happening to children anymore."

"Liddy thought Natalie was being abused again," Tyrell said. "I was so upset when they returned the children to the parents that I drove out to McHenry to see for myself that they were okay. Walked right up to the front door and rang the bell. I do have to say that they had the cleanest house I've ever seen in my life. It didn't look like anybody lived there. Liddy told me that no matter what Natalie said, I should look in her eyes. And I did. Natalie said she was happy and everything was fine, but those little eyes didn't lie. Saddest eyes I've ever seen, with dark circles underneath. I didn't even wait until I got home, called the DCFS hotline from a pay phone. Didn't do any good, though. Time they got there, Natalie was gone."

"Terrible thing," Tyree said.

"Did you both have Natalie in class?" Marti asked.

"No, just Tyrell. I just had the two boys. They were older." Tyree made a face.

"They weren't nice kids," Marti said, hazarding a guess.

"No, they were okay. A little wild, but smart. Big boys, both of them, but not the least bit protective of their sister. One day during recess, one of the other boys was teasing Natalie with a jar of grasshoppers. Natalie just stood there. She looked terrified, but she didn't move. Even when the boy threw the bugs on her hair and they began crawling all over her, she stood still. It was almost as if some part of her wasn't

139

there. And her brothers, there they were with the rest of the kids, taunting and laughing. The oldest actually yelled, 'Go ahead, throw the bugs on her.' When I talked with him about it later, he just laughed. And Natalie was such a sweet little girl," Tyree said.

"She would do anything to please you," Tyrell agreed. "Natalie wanted to be a little girl. The transition from kindergarten to first grade was difficult, becoming a second grader even more so. She was happiest in first grade, and she worked at that level, even though she was bright enough to do better. Her sweetness was very touching, but also very immature. Sometimes, Liddy just let Natalie sit on her lap and she cuddled her. When I told her I thought that might not be the best thing for Natalie, all she said was, 'She needs to feel safe and be loved.' After that, I never said a word."

"Did Liddy ever mention having any children of her own?" Marti asked.

"Liddy?" Tyrell said. "No. I'm sure she didn't."

"She wasn't much for telling people her business, but the way she loved children? She would have talked about something like that," Tyree agreed.

"And you don't know of any family?"

"No. I don't think there was anyone," Tyrell said.

"What about a funeral?" Tyrell asked. "Who's making the arrangements?"

"Nobody, ma'am," Marti said.

"How can we help?"

"I'm not sure. I can let you know as soon as we determine whether there's any next of kin."

"Yes, please, do that," Tyrell said. "If you don't find anyone, we can do something. No way she should just leave here un-mourned."

Marti smiled. They had finally found someone who was Liddy Fields's friend.

By nine o'clock that night, Marti was taking a late swim with Ben and the boys. She and Joanna had had an interesting conversation an hour earlier.

"Guess what," she said to Ben as they sat on the sand and watched boats bobbing in the darkness.

"I give."

"Joanna gave us permission to sleep to-gether."

Ben threw back his head and laughed until tears came to his eyes. "Scary, isn't it?" he said, when he caught his breath. "I guess I know what we won't be doing this summer."

"I'm not sure what it was really about," Marti said. "Joanna's usually pretty easy to figure out, but this time I'm not sure. She

141

says all of her friends' parents do it, and she doesn't want us to think we'd be setting a bad example."

"I'm sure she's told Chris," Ben said.

"How's that going?"

"He pants from afar, at least when I'm around."

"Which can't be often enough. Maybe I'm pressuring her in another way."

"Maybe it's not the wrong kind of pressure, Marti. When I look at Chris, I think of Mike. How can I expect my son to behave differently if I don't? Maybe Joanna and Chris need the kind of pressure that at least implies responsibility. God, did I say that? These kids are pressuring me."

Marti leaned her head on Ben's shoulder. "I just wish I understood what's going on with her."

"Joanna likes Chris a lot, and she tends to be shy around boys."

"Really?"

"I think so. She needs enough space to develop a little more self-confidence. I think you're giving her that, but maybe, in the back of her mind, giving in to Chris would be easier."

His insight surprised her. If he understood that much about Joanna, how much did he know about her? She jumped up. "How about another swim?"

"And then home," Ben said. "You'll have

time to get a decent night's sleep for a change."

Marti wasn't used to . . . what? Being looked after? Johnny took it for granted that she could take care of herself and let it go at that. Ben was always . . . there. He was more concerned about her than Johnny had been. Did she want that?

"I can take care of myself, Ben Walker."

He gave her a slow, easy smile. "Why Officer Mac, ma'am, you've been doing that for years now."

"And?"

"And I don't think that will ever change."

"So?"

"You get cranky when you don't get enough sleep and you spend too much time away from your kids."

She had spent time with Theo and Joanna twice in two days. It was never easy for her to choose between the job and her family. Maybe work won out too often.

"Come on, Officer Mac. Last one in is a cop."

She beat him to the water.

CHAPTER 14

Warren Admunds came to the precinct early Monday morning and told the officer at the desk that he wanted to make a confession. When Marti and Vik met with him in the interrogation room, Vik maintained eye contact and tried to sound sympathetic when he Mirandized him.

"You understand your rights as I have read them to you?" Vik said.

"Yes. And I don't need a lawyer."

"Sir, I'd prefer it if you didn't waive your right to an attorney."

Warren shook his head. "It won't be necessary. I don't want one."

"Okay." Vik straddled a chair.

"I don't want anyone else to know about this," Warren said. "But they will, won't they? I put the oil there."

"When did you do that, Warren?" Vik asked.

"That night — Wednesday night. I called to talk to her and she wouldn't answer."

"Pretty upset, were you?"

"Yes. I was upset. I couldn't tell her the truth. I couldn't keep covering her living expenses. I was upset."

"What time did you get there?"

"Around midnight."

"Midnight?"

"Yes."

"On the third of July?"

"Wednesday night. Yes."

Marti stared at the strips of hair on Warren's head. Maybe his wife wasn't as stupid as they thought she was when she told them he had left the house. The trip to the store and calls to his brother, Gilbert, took place before he went to his mother's, implying that Warren was at home the rest of the night.

"What happened when you got there?" Vik asked.

One less case, Marti thought. Listening to Warren confess wouldn't give her any pleasure, but it would resolve the Admunds case.

"I, umm, I let myself in through the kitchen door. The light was on in the living room, so I went in there, but she wasn't there. Her tea was there, her book, as if she'd just gotten up for a minute, but she wasn't anywhere in the house. I went to the basement door, and I saw her."

"Saw her?" Vik said. He didn't sound surprised, but Marti was.

"At the bottom of the stairs. I felt for a pulse in her neck. She was already getting cold. She wasn't even warm anymore."

Vik probed for half an hour without getting Warren to admit any more than that.

"I thought she had slipped and fallen, but I was afraid the police — that you wouldn't think so, so I put oil on the step and took a towel and rubbed some on the soles of her shoes. I thought that would help, that you would know what happened when you saw it. Instead . . ."

Marti got up and walked to the table. Leaning against it, she said, "Warren, did you park in the ravine behind your mother's house that Wednesday night?"

Warren stared at her for a minute. "The . . . the . . . ravine?"

"Yes. You said you entered through the kitchen door."

Warren looked at Vik, who shrugged and held out his hands.

"Did you approach your mother's house on foot from the ravine at any time that Wednesday night?"

"No."

"Then why was it necessary to enter through the kitchen door?"

Warren looked at Vik again.

"I think she's got you, Warren," he said. "I think you'd better talk to her."

"I didn't want the old lady to see me, the neighbor across the street. She's a night owl and nosy as hell. I parked a block over and walked back."

146

"Through the ravine?"

"Yes."

"Why didn't you want anyone to see you?"
He stared at her.

"Why, Warren — if you only wanted to talk with your mother?"

"I didn't . . . I wouldn't . . ."

"Hold him," Marti said. "There's no way he went through all that trouble just to talk to her. He knew exactly what he was going to do. That's why he went to the ravine."

"No," Warren said. "No. I told you the truth."

"Right," Marti said. She repeated his story. "What does that sound like to you, Warren? Would you believe that story if I told it to you?"

"But I . . . I . . ." Tears came to his eyes. "She was my mother. I would never hurt her."

"And you expect me to believe that? Why? Because you say so? You've said a lot of things, Warren. You said you didn't go near your mother's house Wednesday night. You said you found her body Friday. You left her alone in that hot house for two days, then swore to God that you'd never been inside, that you thought she must be in there dead because of the smell."

Warren cringed as she spoke.

"You lied repeatedly. Why should I believe you now?"

"Because I'm telling the truth."

"That's what you told me before, Warren, when you were lying."

She was not moved by his tears. They had enough circumstantial evidence to go to the state's attorney and request an indictment. Except for that damned clay. How did it get there? She didn't like loose ends. She had watched too many cases get derailed because of some oddball detail like that. If they could just get a confession. She rubbed her jaw, signaling for Vik to take over.

"Look, son, we understand that these things just happen. Everything just gets out of control."

"I was going to go to Jori," Warren said. "I was going to talk to Mother one more time; then I was going to tell Jori."

"I thought you didn't want your family to know about this, son."

"No, but . . ." He sniffled and wiped his eyes with the back of his hand. "Mother . . . she . . . she had tears in her eyes when I told her the real estate agent was coming. I had never seen her cry before — not even when dad died. I was going to ask her one more time, and if she said no, go to Jori."

Vik talked to him for a while longer without results, then looked at Marti and shrugged. He wasn't ready to hold him.

They got a signed statement and let him go.

It was quiet when Marti and Vik went upstairs. There was a faint, sweet odor of Obsession for Men, but no coffee, no Slim, and no Cowboy.

"They were at roll call," Marti said as she peered into the empty coffeepot. "Maybe they're just sulking."

"Well, Lupe's got court, so I don't think the idiots got in over their heads again," Vik said. "Don't bother making any coffee, Mac-Alister. Yesterday's was more than enough. We can make do with this." He got out a jar of instant and a hot pot that he kept for emergencies.

"Warren and Gilbert, damned fools, both of them," he said as he searched for an unused socket. "It's an embarrassment having sons like that."

"But I didn't do it," Marti said, mimicking Warren's high-pitched nervousness. "Me, neither," she added in Gilbert's monotone.

"I'm not sure if I'm holding out for a confession or if I'm just not quite convinced," Vik said. "Warren is serving himself up on a silver platter. Unfortunately, I know that people really can be that stupid."

Marti didn't understand her reluctance to arrest Warren, either. Trust your instincts, Johnny would have said. Her instincts said to wait. "Warren is making it so damned easy for us that I almost feel sorry for him. Almost." She checked the ceramic coffee cup that Joanna had given her a couple of years ago. Coffee had dried at the bottom, but not enough to require a trip to the sink. She wiped it out with a Kleenex.

"If this case comes down to a teaspoon of soil and half a cup of cooking oil, Marti, we could be in trouble. The only suspects we've got are an economist and a college professor. Nobody knows what an economist does. If interest rates are low, he's a good guy; if they're high, he isn't. Professors tend to get respect, if only for being smart.

"And we don't know if Warren's wife was being clever or stupid when she blew their alibis. Hell, maybe they're all in on it, or just looking out for one another, so Warren came in this morning to draw attention away from Gilbert. As far as I'm concerned, either of them could have pushed their mother down a flight of stairs."

Vik measured instant coffee into his cup and added boiling water, then did the same with Marti's mug. Marti tasted hers — she'd give it to the spider plant. She had had seven hours of sleep the night before and now felt alert enough to hold out for some that was freshly brewed. When she went through her incoming reports, she found one on the soil and pollen samples.

"Well, they couldn't tie the clay and pollen to any of the sites involved, not here or in Champaign."

"Damn." Vik scanned the investment portfolio that Gilbert had given him. "From the looks of this, Gilbert was much smarter when it came to money than his big brother the economist." He drummed his fingers on the desk. "The thing here is the dynamics — how the old woman would have reacted once she knew Warren blew all of the cash and there was nothing for her old age, and how she would have felt when she found out that Gilbert had sold her jewels for more than enough to take care of her for the rest of her life."

Marti thought of the furniture and mementos crammed into those four small rooms, then compared that with jewels stored at a bank. "My guess is that the house would have come first, and Warren would have been totally out of favor."

The finger tapping stopped. "So," Vik said, "older brother was about to get shown up by younger brother. All those years that Warren was top dog were about to end and Gilbert was going to one-up him. And not only was little brother going to be the hero but Warren was going to look like a complete ass. There's always the possibility that Gilbert did it, but my money is on Warren. Poor Gilbert, he came this close to the

151

payback of a lifetime."

Vik spoke with such vehemence that Marti wondered which of his two older brothers he would like to one-up.

CHAPTER 15

By the time Marti parked in front of Alma Miller's trailer just before three, the temperature was 101° F. The trailer park was just north of Lincoln Prairie. Mature oaks and maples shaded the trailers that squatted in parallel lines on grassy lots along the paved roads. Alma's trailer had a porch with a roof. A variety of rosebushes lined both sides of the short walk to the front steps, and their fragrance perfumed the air.

"Why Detective MacAlister," Alma said when she opened the door. "I didn't think anyone in the police department would pay the least bit of attention to me. Even my sister thinks I'm a little touched when I tell her about my dreams."

Marti felt like a giant entering a dollhouse as she walked into Alma's kitchen. Even though the interior was roomier than she expected, she felt claustrophobic.

"Come to the kitchen. I just made a pot of coffee about an hour ago. Darred didn't wake me and so I slept late this morning. I used to get up at four when we was farming. Seven-thirty seems like the middle of the day."

Marti sat on a stool facing a window almost the width of the trailer. Small pots of herbs were arranged on the windowsill.

Alma folded paper napkins and put spoons on them, then took a sugar bowl out of the refrigerator. "Nothing like getting it right from the cows," she said as she filled a small pitcher with milk. She put two thick mugs of coffee on the counter and sat on the stool next to Marti's.

"My son just started a small herb garden this summer," Marti said. Theo was growing something along the perimeters of the vegetable garden that he hoped would keep the rabbits away.

"There's no place to grow things here," Alma said. "Except for those pots. Not that I miss it like I thought I would. A lot of work. There's something special about bringing vegetables from the field to the table, though. Nothing you can buy in the store tastes anything like it."

"How long has it been since you lived on a farm?"

"Oh, it's been close to ten years now. Seems longer. Darred works at Lamb's Farm now, helping with the animals. Things worked out good for him. He always did like working with animals better than he liked farming."

"Did you have these dreams when you were on the farm?" Marti asked.

"I've had these dreams ever since I was a little girl," Alma said. "The first one I can remember that might've meant something was when I was floating in this black water and couldn't get out. I wasn't afraid or nothing. I just kept floating along and couldn't swim to the top. Next day, everyone was talking about a neighbor boy who drowned in the creek. It was spring. The creek flooded its banks because of the rain."

"How do you know when a dream is . . . different?"

Alma blew on her coffee, then took a sip and put the mug down. She added more milk. "Most often, I don't. I can't really tell unless I hear about something that sounds similar. Lots of times, I can't connect it with nothing."

"Do you dream often?"

"It kind of goes in streaks. I won't dream nothing for months maybe. Then all of a sudden, there might be two, three of them."

"When I was growing up," Marti said, "there were women in my neighborhood who had different kinds of . . . gifts. Women who could 'see,' as we called it. I'm not sure how some of them knew what they did, if it came to them in dreams or not, but most

155

often they were right. Do you just have dreams?"

"Far as I know."

"If, for example, you were to touch something that belonged to Liddy Fields or went where she lived, would you experience anything else?"

Alma seemed troubled by the question. "This ain't like nothing I ever saw on TV. I don't never know no more than what the dreams tell me, and most all of the time, I can't even figure that out." She reached across the counter and picked at one of the herb plants, then sat back, releasing the scent of spearmint as she crushed the leaves in her hand.

"All my life, I've been trying not to have these dreams. Sometimes . . ." Moisture gathered in her eyes as she stared out the window. "This ain't something that I want to do. Sometimes I wake up knowing someone's been hurt real bad, that there was so much pain . . . or fear. . . . It ain't never nothing good that's happening to them. And it ain't just the pain that I feel. They have feelings when it's happening — terrible feelings." She wiped her eyes. "I don't want to have these dreams. I try real hard not to. I've got it so now I hardly ever have one, and I like that. Sometimes, like with Liddy . . ." She paused and began to shiver. "I don't like knowing who it is, either."

Marti looked outside. A bee hovered near the window. Unlike Alma, the women she knew years ago were comfortable with their ability to see. They were esteemed by the community and well acquainted with their gifts. Although they couldn't make something happen, they did know what to do that might induce a dream or call something to mind.

"Did Liddy have these feelings you describe?" Marti asked.

Alma put her hands to her face. After what seemed like a long while, she said, "I have to make myself do this." A few minutes later, she said, "She was soothed by the water. Something inside needed healing. She wasn't afraid — not until . . . whatever happened." Hunching forward, she began to cry.

Marti put her arm about Alma's shoulders. "Liddy didn't just drown. Somebody killed her. And you might still know something that can help me find out who that was. Please don't try to shut out whatever dreams or memories you might have. Please let them come through. Whoever killed her might kill again. And even if they don't, Liddy deserves justice. Like it or not, you have a gift. I need you to use it."

Alma went to the sink and splashed water on her face. "Ain't never thought of it as that before," she said, reaching for a dish towel. "It has sure never seemed like no gift to know how people die." She sniffed. "On TV, they give someone some clothes or something and all of a sudden they seem to get these feelings or these pictures in their minds. I don't ever want to be able to do nothing like that. I don't want to be able to do this." She turned to Marti. "This seems to be perfectly normal to you."

"I grew up around women like you," Marti said. "They were good women, all of them. I never heard one of them say why she thought she was given her gift. But they all seemed to think they had a responsibility to use it."

Alma turned away. "Sometimes, there's something that connects the dreams. I'm never sure why or what, but I just kind of know. There was something about this dream. It was connected to something I've dreamed before. It had something to do with a child. I've dreamed every night since I talked with you. But they aren't like . . . those dreams. I can remember only bits and pieces. My husband usually writes my dreams in a journal, but he hasn't bothered to write down any of these."

"Tell me about them."

"Oh, there's a big empty house without windows, and some funny kind of stars that weren't real but were shining until the light went on. A couple were just noises — animal sounds, the roar of the ocean, a strong wind. I feel stupid telling you about them. They aren't connected to anything. They don't mean anything. They're just dreams."

"How often do you have these kinds of dreams?"

"Oh, I don't unless I've had one of the bad ones. Darred thinks it's things from the bad dreams that I don't want to remember that get all jumbled up and become something I don't mind thinking about. He thinks maybe things like laughter might really be crying but that I can't stand to think about it, so it becomes something I don't mind remembering. Does any of that make sense?"

"Oh yes," Marti said. "I knew a woman who had dreams and some of them brought her a great deal of peace. She didn't just have the bad dreams."

Alma rubbed the back of one hand with her thumb. "I've never seen any use for my dreams, or understood them."

"When my father died," Marti said, "he was porter on a train somewhere between Kansas City, Missouri, and St. Louis. My mother was upset because he died alone. Then Miss Rosetta Grey came over. She usually knew when someone was going to die. She told my mother that she didn't say anything when she sensed it might be Poppa's time, because there was such a

159

feeling of peace surrounding him that she thought she was wrong. I can't tell you how much that comforted my mother."

Alma thought about that for a few minutes, then sighed deeply. "I won't promise you anything, Detective MacAlister, but for a while, at least, I won't do none of those things I usually do to keep from dreaming again, just in case there is some good to be found in it."

It was close to 5:30 when Marti pulled up across the street from the motel. A stocky gray-haired woman took her to Liddy's room. The stars on the ceiling were gone. There was a ladder in one corner. A paint-splattered rag hung from one of the rungs. Several cans of paint were on the floor, and the room smelled of it and turpentine. The ceiling was white; two walls and part of a third were a pale yellow.

"This is my room now," the woman said. "Those stars that were up there made it look like a child's room. No children here."

Marti thought of what Alma had said about stars that weren't real but shined until the light went on. She wondered what other fragments of reality might be jumbled up in Alma's dreams.

CHAPTER 16

Ben called almost as soon as Marti got back to the precinct. Joanna would be throwing out the opening pitch in five minutes. Marti hadn't even begun writing the day's notes. When she hesitated about going to the game, Vik insisted. She was going to spend time with her children. She was beginning to think Vik and the lieutenant were in on this together.

Joanna's team remained undefeated. After the game, Marti helped Ben spread a table-cloth on a picnic table in the park. Theo and Mike took a cooler out of the van and announced dinner.

"Nothing fancy," Ben said. "Sub sandwiches and salads and a couple of six-packs of iced tea."

"Vegetarian subs?"

"No. But Joanna has got me eating healthier than I used to. I've lost seven pounds."

Marti thought Ben looked just right the way he was — big, but lean. "You're not fat anywhere, and I sort of like you the way you are. Stand up for a minute."

She looked him up and down. "I guess it's okay."

Ben winked at her and called the boys to the table.

"Is this real meat," Theo asked, "or that turkey stuff?"

"Turkey stuff," Ben said.

"Yuck."

"No, look," Ben said. He opened the sandwich. "Pickles, tomatoes, olives, cheese, bell peppers. Great stuff."

"You sound like Joanna," Theo said. "I'm skipping the salad."

Mike, who was at least fifteen pounds heavier than Theo and not more than half a head taller, reached for a sandwich and a salad without complaint.

Ben said grace. As they ate, the Lincoln Prairie Symphony Orchestra began setting up for an outdoor concert.

"I've got to get back pretty soon," Marti said.

"It looked to me like Vik had things pretty well under control."

"I suppose."

"You're wired tonight. How come?"

"I'm not wired."

"Marti, you're jiggling your foot; you've stood up and sat down five times —"

"Twice," Marti said, interrupting him.

"And you're looking around as if you ex-

162

pect someone to open up with an AK-forty-seven."

"Habit. I'm a cop."

He reached across the table and took her hands in his. "A rather attractive cop. A cop who is stressed-out. Now, I've got some lawn chairs. Joanna and Chris are coming by. Let's just give it another hour. Just one hour with me and the kids."

Surprised by her eagerness to get back to the precinct and catch up on paperwork, Marti reluctantly agreed.

Reaching out, she took Ben's hand. "Thanks for thinking of this. I need a break." The orchestra began to play. Marti tried to concentrate.

"Tchaikovsky," she said after a few minutes.

"How can you tell?"

"The way the wind instruments play and the way the mood changes." Not the kind of music she listened to very often, but she always found Tchaikovsky reassuring. His music seemed to imply that even a hundred years ago, life could go from calm to chaotic in a millisecond.

CHAPTER 17

The sun had just come up when Tyrell Laws set off for her morning walk. She always arrived early enough to be the only person on the trail. It was her favorite time of day. Even when she was teaching, she got up every day and did two circuits on the local jogging trail. Only blinding snow, electrical storms, and driving rain kept her indoors. Days like today were her favorites. The sun was low in the east; the sky was a bright, clear blue; the grass glistened with dew; the birds twittered wake-up calls; insects hummed; tall grasses rustled as small creatures crept about. Tyrell inhaled deeply as she walked. There was something almost euphoric about the lavishness God endowed upon a new day. She thought Eve must have felt like this when Adam first awakened her.

"Lord, I love the beauty of your house," she said aloud. "The tenting place of your glory."

A sudden squabble of sparrows jolted her. She felt a sharp pain across the front of her ankle and held out her hands as she fell forward. Before she could get to her feet, someone reached down to help her. Strong hands pulled her toward the side of the road.

"I can manage now." She turned to see who it was. "Why . . ."

Before she could say anything else, he grabbed a handful of hair. He pulled her head back, then pushed it forward.

Marti got a call from Tyree Laws while she was in a meeting with the lieutenant. When she called back, Tyree was hysterical.

"Dead?" Marti said. "Tyrell is dead?" They had just spoken with her Sunday afternoon. "What happened? . . . She was out walking? Who's there with you?" As soon as she determined that Tyree was not alone, she contacted the Racine detective assigned to death investigations. The autopsy was scheduled for three o'clock.

"They must not have much to do," Vik said.

"It sounds more like there's not much happening in Chicago. Racine has a part-time forensic pathologist who works in Cook County. He's going to take the afternoon off."

"Maybe he just wants to take a break from gunshot victims. How is Racine calling this? Unofficially."

"Unofficially, their man thinks Laws's

death looks suspicious. They've got a tech at the scene now."

"Let's go."

"Jessenovik, you can get away with aggravating the hell out of our guys, but this jurisdiction isn't even in the same state."

As Marti and Vik walked two miles along the perimeter of the preserve, Marti paid little attention to the flowers and foliage, as she would have if Theo had been along. A quarter of a mile in, her blouse was damp with sweat and sticking to her back. Sand and gravel crunched beneath her feet. The hum of the cicadas rose and fell in uneven waves. She flicked at small clouds of mosquitoes, swatting at those that landed on her neck.

"There they are," Vik said.

Ahead, she could see a car parked along the edge of the trail and two uniforms. When they identified themselves, a third officer scrabbled out from under a stand of dense bushes and identified himself as the tech.

"You from Lincoln Prairie?"

He grinned when they introduced themselves. "This tie in with something you've got?"

"We were talking with the victim Sunday about a case we've got," Vik said.

"Think that's got anything to do with

this?" the tech asked.

"Can't see how," Vik answered.

Marti wasn't sure she agreed.

"Take a look under here," the tech said. Marti crawled under the bushes with him, about eight feet in, to the one with the thickest trunk.

"See?" He pointed to a circular pattern of little chinks about five inches from the base. "Now, come over here." She scooted out. Vik followed.

The trunk of the tree almost directly across from the scrubs had similar marks. There weren't many and they weren't deep. In some places, there was barely a scratch. There were none where the bark was rough.

An older man joined them. He wore wire-rimmed glasses and had a mustache. He held out his hand. "Mark Rigby." He was the local officer Marti had spoken to over the phone. "My guess is that someone tied something to the trees so she would trip. The chipping pattern suggests something that would bite rather than rub, maybe an eighth-of-an-inch-thick wire."

"Did the fall kill her?"

"No," Rigby said. He pointed to a large rock. Marti could see blood and brain matter.

"Take a look here."

There were drag marks leading to the rock. Following them, they could see where

the rock had been. The insect activity indicated that the rock had been moved quite
recently.

"We've got weight indentations in the
grass, but there's nothing here to hold a
footprint. Our man also picked up bits of
fibers from the branches." Rigby stroked his
mustache. It made Marti think of Tyree at
home with the cat.

"Just so you know, one of the woman's
fingernails was broken and we got some
skin samples, so our perp might have a few
scratches. Other than that, there were no
defense wounds. It must have happened
pretty fast. No one here that time of morning, so even if she screamed, nobody would
have heard her. Oh, and the sister said she
would have had some jewelry on — a watch,
and maybe a gold chain she always wore,
and a ring. Only thing she had when we
found her were gold studs in her ears."

"Tyrell Laws and Liddy Fields reported
Natalie Beatty's abuse," Marti said as they
returned to the car.

Vik waved away a swarm of gnats and
walked ahead of her. "The Beatty case was
a nightmare," he said as Marti started the
car.

"How so?"

"The kid was abused. She has never been
found. Nobody has ever been arrested. It

168

was out of my jurisdiction. There was nothing I could do. Doesn't that sound like a
damned nightmare to you?"

Marti understood how he felt. She cringed
inside every time the victim was a child.

"We're going to have to take a look at this,
Vik. Make a few inquiries."

"Sounds far-fetched to me. That kid's
been missing seven years now. Why in the
hell, after all of this time, would anyone
bother killing Fields and Laws?"

"Because they reported the abuse."

"But why now?"

"Maybe we'll find out."

Marti called Denise Stevens, a juvenile
officer, to find out who had been involved
with the Beatty case. To her surprise, two
hours later a large manila folder was hand-
delivered, along with the name, address,
and telephone number of the detective who
had headed up the investigation. He had
since left the force but was still in the area,
and he was willing to see Marti and Vik.

Ed Morgan was a young man, not more
than thirty-five. Marti and Vik sat on a dock
on Fox Lake and watched as half a dozen
children splashed and swam in the water.
The sun was dipping in the west, but it
would be another two hours until dark.

"The two towheads are mine by birth,"
Morgan said. "The others are either adopted
or foster kids. After what happened to

Natalie, I realized I was on the wrong end of things. This is where you have to begin. I'm a teacher now — third grade."

The grade Natalie would have been entering when she disappeared.

"What can you tell us about the case?" Vik asked.

"Not enough to nail the bastard or even figure out where they buried her."

"Why are you so certain that she's dead?" Marti asked.

"Because for seven years they abused her. They withheld food; they made her eat dog food and cat food; they made her drink milk with salt or vinegar in it. She weighed forty-one pounds when she was seven years old. I haven't seen photographs like that since Biafra."

"Who do you think did it?"

"Probably the father, Joe. Doreen seemed too timid to do anything, but she could have. That woman was so eager to please him that I actually watched her get him a can of pop when he held out his hand, and open it for him. He didn't have to say a word."

"What about the two boys?"

"God knows what they knew. They were all just too calm, too quiet, all of them. And they all had the same story, never deviated by one word: The real father had called two days before. Natalie went to bed that night and when they woke up the next morning, she was gone. The room she was supposed to have slept in — there was nothing there but a bed. They had thrown a mat away, like the one she slept on before the state took her, but they denied she was sleeping on it. There were pet-food dishes in the trash, empty cans of pet food. They claimed they had a puppy and a kitten but that it was too much work and so they abandoned them along the side of the road. Lies, all of it, but not one damned thing we could prove. No circumstantial evidence at all."

Morgan skipped a stone across the water. "Nobody ever saw her. The neighbors didn't even know she lived there. And that story about another man being her father — she was the youngest child, looked just like Joe Beatty. His name was on the birth certificate, but all of a sudden she wasn't his. They lied! And Joe Beatty, looking at me with those dead-fish eyes, daring me to prove it, and I couldn't."

Morgan shook his head. "It haunts me. I wake up at night thinking about that house. It was so immaculate, you couldn't believe anyone lived there. Everything in the cabinets stacked just so, same with the refrigerator. Clothing arranged with military precision." He shuddered. "Scary. I know damned good and well they killed her."

CHAPTER 18

Marti and Vik went to see Lieutenant Dirkowitz right after roll call Wednesday morning. The lieutenant was standing with his back to them, looking out at a hazy sky. He cleared his throat a few times and coughed. "I got a call from McHenry last night," he said. "You made some inquiries about the Natalie Beatty case. They're de-lighted. You've got their full cooperation. What have you got?" He sounded con-gested. Allergies, Marti decided as he sat down.

"Maybe nothing," Vik cautioned.

"Or?"

"Liddy Fields reported the abuse that re-sulted in the Beatty children being placed in foster care," Vik said.

"And," Marti added, "there was a homicide in Racine yesterday. We had talked with the woman on Sunday. She reported abuse just before Natalie disappeared."

The lieutenant's eyes narrowed.

"I know, sir," Vik said. "It's been a little too long for revenge."

"We don't know that, Jessenovik," the

172

lieutenant said. "And we don't know what happened to that little girl." He picked up the hand grenade. "It was outside of our jurisdiction, but if we could find out what happened to her . . . What do you know about Fields?"

"Not much," Marti admitted. "Fields worked in schools for years. Apparently, she was upset by Natalie's disappearance." A school photo in the reports showed a pretty child with pink bows in straight dark hair and a wobbly smile. Marti's stomach tensed as she thought of the photograph. Those sad dark eyes would keep her awake at night.

"And?" the lieutenant prompted.

"Fields stopped working with children a year later. Unfortunately, although it seems she was a great talker, she never told anyone much about herself, with the exception of the woman we talked with on Sunday. As for knowing anything about Natalie's disappearance . . . it seems unlikely that there could be any connection after all this time. The only odd coincidence we've come across so far is the death in Racine. That's the only reason we're looking into the case."

Vik sucked in his breath. "This isn't about Natalie Beatty. And this isn't about Tyrell Laws, either. This is about Liddy Fields. I resent being dragged into the Beatty case just because Fields knew her. It has noth-

173

ing to do with why Fields died."

"We don't know that," Marti said.

"Oh, the hell we don't. You just want to find out what happened to the kid. Well, I don't."

"Pursue it," the lieutenant said, dropping the grenade.

Thunder was rumbling by the time Marti returned to her desk. The wind picked up and a chain clanked against the flagpole outside the window. "Maybe we'll get some relief from this heat."

"Or the rain will increase the humidity," Vik said.

"We need to agree on where we're going with this, Jessenovik. The lieutenant wants us to follow up on any Beatty leads."

"We are going to find out who killed Fields. If, in the process, that somehow impinges on the Beatty case, fine."

"Two people involved with that case are dead."

"Coincidence," Vik said.

"Convince me." She was as wary of coincidences as he was.

Marti took out the Beatty file. She forced herself to look at Natalie's picture again, felt her stomach lurch, then slipped the photo into an envelope.

"This was a very detailed, point-in-time investigation," she told Vik. "There is very little background information. The parents

174

were born and raised in a small town just outside of Peoria. There was an extensive search for Natalie there. The father, Joe Beatty, went to college in De Kalb; the mother didn't go anywhere until she married him two years after he graduated and moved here. Everything else focuses on Natalie's disappearance. There was an intensive search in McHenry and also in Peoria. Nothing was ever found."

Vik walked to the window, both hands jammed in his pockets. "A lot of man-hours went into the Beatty case. It's frustrating as hell to do everything right and still come up empty."

There was a crackle of lightning and a boom of thunder before rain began pelting the window. When Marti passed the reports to Vik, he put them in his hold basket.

At five after nine, Marti called Denise Stevens. "You've got my attention," Denise said. "If we could finally find out what happened to that child. It's one of those cases that just stays with you." Catholic Charities and DCFS had records on the family that Marti might be allowed to see, possibly without a subpoena. The family court records were sealed, but Denise knew someone who had been involved with the case who might have some informal notes.

Marti called the agencies involved, then began the legal process of getting the records released. She reached for the Beatty file. The pages rustled. Lightning flashed. Rain drummed against the window. The chain outside kept clanking. When Marti noticed a steady ache between her shoulder blades, she realized she was hunched over her desk, and she straightened up.

Half an hour later, Denise called back. "I might have something better than notes. The social worker from Catholic Charities will talk with you, off the record."

When Marti told Vik, he swore and snapped a pencil in half. "It was eight days before they called off the search for that kid. They didn't find a trace of her, not even a sock, nothing. If they couldn't find anything then, what do you think we can find after seven years? Fields died ten days ago. Look at how far we've gotten with that case."

Vik ran his fingers through his wiry hair. It became even more unruly. The overhead light played on the silver strands. "I don't think I want to know what happened to Natalie Beatty," he said. "I think I'd rather just believe she's somewhere, okay?"

The weariness in Vik's voice caught Marti off guard. Vik hadn't taken as much time off as she had the past couple of days, hadn't spent as much time with his family.

"Why don't you go home early today?" she said. "I've been taking time off to be with the kids. Maybe you need an evening with your wife."

"We'll see."

The rain had stopped by the time Marti and Vik went to meet Compania Ortega, the social worker, for lunch at a Tex-Mex restaurant. Vik was right. It was overcast, hotter, and muggy. Ortega was a short, slender, middle-aged woman with straight black hair cut in bangs just above her eyebrows.

As the waiter brought mugs of iced tea, Ortega said, "I didn't have much contact with this family. I just assisted in finding a foster home. We try to keep the children together, and I work very hard to find families that will accept multiple placements. Natalie was seven. She had two older brothers — Max was nine and Vaughn was eleven. I took them to the foster home."

"Did you have any contact with the parents?"

"I did go to the home to pick up some of the children's belongings." Ortega opened a packet of sweetener and stirred it into the tea. "I think that was when I understood. According to the DCFS caseworker, Natalie described the abuse the way any other child would talk about ordinary care. It was normal to her. The parents denied that there was any abuse, and the siblings agreed.

177

Everybody involved was divided over who was telling the truth. This was a middle-class family. The father was a college graduate and had an excellent job. What really made the case difficult was that there were no signs of physical abuse — no scars or healed fractures, no bruises. It was scary to me to think that child abuse had become so sophisticated that it could be this difficult to prove. One thing I can tell you that is not documented is that Joe Beatty lost his job because of this. Officially, there was some other reason, just so he couldn't sue. They recruited him while he was in college and he went right into management training. His expertise was in tool-and-die making. I don't know much about that except that people with that kind of background are getting scarce, and you can make a lot of money at it. Joe didn't have too much trouble finding another job after we placed the children. I don't think he was high in management, but they moved to McHenry and were still doing well when the children were returned. Natalie's disappearance took care of that job, and apparently Joe didn't fit the 'corporate image' anymore. The last I heard, he was a foreman."

The food came. Marti looked at Ortega's healthy bowl of greens and chicken and vegetables, then at the cheddar cheese that was melted over her own beef, pork, and bacon sandwich. She wondered what it would do to her cholesterol count, then chided herself for being concerned. Joanna had been in the kitchen when she got up this morning and they had bagels with fat-free cream cheese. Just because Joanna was worried that Marti would keel over with a heart attack was no reason to give in to Joanna's dietary demands. It was bad enough that Joanna was winning Ben over.

"What happened when you went to their house?" Marti asked.

"They met me at the front door. Everything was packed in boxes. I went through everything before taking it to the children. There were toys for the boys but not for Natalie. She had beautiful clothes, but not one toy. Nothing. I thought maybe they were getting back at her for telling on them. I got her a Barbie doll and a dollhouse. It took the foster mother three days to convince Natalie that it was okay to play with them, that the toys were hers to keep. She had never had any toys of her own."

"Was Natalie the only Beatty child abused?" Marti hated cases like that. There was always something bizarre about the near normalcy surrounding the other children.

"Yes," Ortega said. "But there's no easy answer as to why. Any one of them could have been singled out by the parents."

"Either parent?"

"Or both. Doreen was abused herself as a child. Joe came from an abusive family also. Although Doreen denied it, the odds are that Joe was abusing her as well as Natalie. Natalie was obviously malnourished. Doreen was gaunt."

"Is Joe a big man?" Marti asked.

"No. He's five eight, maybe. But I could see that he and the two boys ate well."

"Why did the Beattys get the children back?"

"Unfortunately, the parents complied with everything the court required and were pronounced rehabilitated. Of course, Max and Vaughn wanted to go home. They resented authority, did not like having rules, and were not used to having to treat their sister with any respect. If Natalie had come to everyone's attention with healed fractures and inadequately explained scars, if she had been raped or beaten, perhaps it would not have been so easy. And then, when she disappeared . . ."

Vik was pushing french fries around his plate, but he wasn't eating. Marti wasn't hungry, either. The waiter refilled their mugs.

Ortega pushed her plate away, food hardly touched. "Eight years ago last June, I took them to the foster home. We stopped for ice cream on the way. Then, there were so many cases, I forgot about them. A year later, they were back home and within six weeks Natalie was gone. Now I never forget."

"Do you know what happened to them?"

"Once they left the foster home, it was DCFS's responsibility. We didn't do any further follow-up." Ortega sighed. "There is so much to do, so many children to help, so many people. Sometimes you aren't able to do very much. But this . . . never to know what happened to that child. If there is anything else I can do to help . . . Denise says you're going to find out."

Marti looked at Vik. He balled up his napkin and threw it on his plate. Denise was an optimist.

Half an hour after Marti and Vik returned to the precinct, Denise Stevens came in. She was a big woman, Marti's height but about fifteen pounds heavier. Unlike Marti, she was not pleased with her size, and she used hats to divert attention away from her hips, so people would concentrate on her face. She had doe-shaped eyes and pecan brown skin and a dimpled smile.

"Lord, but it has gotten even more humid out there, if that's possible. It must be near a hundred percent. And it looks like it might be going to rain again." She draped a voluminous raincoat over the back of a chair and took off a floppy wide-brimmed hat made of the same shiny black fabric. An umbrella was wedged in the side pocket of her large purse. She pulled a chair midway between Vik's desk and Marti's. "So, you two are working on the Beatty case. That's a break."

"For who?" Vik asked.

"Natalie."

"Not if she's dead."

"I know, Jessenovik. And I'm sure you don't want to touch this. But a lot of people would like to give it some closure, whatever happened."

"We've got other cases that are a lot more recent and should have a higher priority."

"Why Vik, I'd thought you'd jump right on this one. Nobody in McHenry County could solve it when it happened. If you could pull it off seven years later . . ."

Vik stood up. "I think I'll go get a pop. Can I get you one?" He banged the door shut on his way out.

"I think he protests too much," Denise said. "And your nose is sure twitching."

Marti rubbed the edge of the envelope where she had put Natalie's school picture. "This could have come at a better time."

"If things were too quiet, it might take the edge off."

"You've been around cops too long."

Denise had one sister in alcohol rehab

and another in a mental institution. "How's your mother?" Marti asked, playing it safe.

"Momma's fine. And Belle is sober, working part-time and singing in a church choir."

When Denise didn't say anything about her younger sister, Terri, Marti assumed she wasn't doing as well.

"And Zaar?" She was Terri's little girl.

"Momma is so good with Zaar. I think it's a second chance for her to do what she couldn't do with us."

Vik came back with cans of pop and bags of chips. "Too bad we're not British bobbies. They get to have beer with lunch. I could use one right about now."

Denise ignored the chips and chose the only can of diet soda. "I tried to do a little sniffing around for you, see who I knew and if I could expedite things, but I hit a brick wall. The only other person I could come up with who might have helped out died last November."

Marti exchanged looks with Vik. She filled Denise in on the potential connection between the Beatty case and Fields's and Laws's deaths.

"The person I mentioned died of cancer," Denise said. "I visited her in the hospital for over a month. When she finally went, it was a blessing."

"You had me worried for a minute,

Stevens," Vik said. "One or two victims, and somebody is a little ticked off. More than that and we've got a time bomb on our hands."

CHAPTER 19

There was a fresh pot of coffee perking when Marti arrived at the precinct Thursday morning. "Is the strike over?" she asked. "Have the Testosterone Twosome resolved their differences with Lupe?"

"I think they're either avoiding or just missing one another," Vik said. "They've all been in and out of court this week."

He paged through the Beatty file. "There's not much here." While he was reading, Marti got on the phone again and conveyed the urgency of getting copies of the other reports. She went through Lupe's notes. There was no response to the sketch of Fields that ran in the Tennessee newspapers. There hadn't been any more phone calls. When she talked with detectives in Racine, they had no developments to report. Marti set about trying to find the Beattys, incurring a few debts along the way but coming up empty.

"Nothing," she said. "I can't find them. Joe and Doreen Beatty, and both boys, Max and Vaughn. It's as if they disappeared off the face of the earth, just like Natalie. The last

185

job Joe Beatty had was in a factory four years ago. He got laid off and collected unemployment. That ran out two and a half years ago. Their address then was an SRO in Chicago. There's no record of employment or residency since."

"What about the kids?"

"The youngest, Max, graduated from a junior high school in Chicago two years ago. There's no record of high school enrollment or of a transfer to a school out of the city."

"Don't they send out truant officers anymore?"

"I don't think so. Besides, they'd have to know he was truant. As far as I know, there's no tracking system in Chicago to identify who drops out between eighth grade and high school."

"And the other kid?"

"Vaughn. He dropped out, too."

"And they just vanished?"

"Looks that way," Marti said.

Vik fumed over that for a few minutes. "Well, thanks to McHenry, we can contact members of the family, but if the Beattys are in touch, too . . . if one of them is involved in this and they get an inkling that we're onto them, we'll never find them. There was a search just west of Peoria, too — farm country. Now if that's where they took Natalie, no wonder she was never found. The Beattys must have known that area well, all the hiding places." Vik thumbed through the report. "We could talk to the cop who was in charge of the search in Peoria."

"You handle it," Marti said. "I've been on the phone all morning."

"He suggested we talk to Beatty's uncle," Vik said when he hung up. "I never heard of the town." He took out a state map. "Looks almost midway between Peoria and Galesburg. What's that, a four- or five-hour drive?"

"I thought we just agreed that talking with relatives might not be a good idea."

"This guy says half the family's not speaking to the other half, that this uncle can at least give us some background."

"And then the uncle tells the aunt, who calls the cousin, who calls the friend, who —"

"Look, Marti, this a small-town thing; the cop I talked to is a small-town cop. He knows the politics, the personalities."

"I guess I'll have to take your word for that, Jessenovik. Anyone old enough to remember Lincoln Prairie when it was a town of thirty-five thousand knows a lot more about things like that than I do."

"Information," Vik said. "We need information. We can't do much of anything without it. Someone's got to talk to us. I'll drive down. If we leave now, we can get there by

187

five or six tonight. You handle the drive back."

"Six o'clock? I thought farmers went to bed before sundown."

"These people are old, Marti. Old people don't sleep at all, hardly. It's a hell of a way to waste time when you haven't got much of it left."

Marti grabbed her purse and followed him out the door. It was a relief to have something to do.

They couldn't find the house and the Beattys had no telephone. After a half hour of driving up and down the same roads, past barns and cows and corn, Vik called the local police and got directions. The house was on a small lot wedged between two multiacre cornfields. They had passed the turnoff at least twice.

"Rustic," Marti said as they turned onto a gravel road. Geese scattered in their path.

"The birds are up a bit late, aren't they, Vik?"

"I wouldn't know."

"Maybe they're old."

"At least it doesn't smell of manure around here, MacAlister."

An arthritic dog hobbled down the steps of a sagging porch as they pulled up in front of the white wood-framed house.

A man came to the door with a shotgun.

188

Marti snapped her holster open and took out her shield. "Real rustic," she muttered as she rolled down the window. "Police, sir. Can we talk with you for a minute?"

The man stood at least six feet tall. His hair was white, his face was weathered and tan, and he looked at least seventy-five. He kept the gun barrel pointed down, but Marti didn't doubt his ability to swing the weapon up and get off a round before she could unholster her Beretta.

"Police," she said again, and held up her shield.

The man took a step forward.

"Don't come any closer with the shotgun," she warned.

The man gave her a toothless grin and said, "Hey, Opal, Don said we might have some city cops calling. I guess this is them."

The woman who came to the door was at least a foot shorter, but her face was as weathered and she looked just as old. She took the shotgun inside.

Marti and Vik sat in creaking wicker rockers on the front porch with Harry Beatty while Opal made a pitcher of iced tea. The geese chased about the grass, with their long necks close to the ground, catching low-flying insects.

"Got us a couple of bats, too," Harry said. "Don't have to worry none about mosquitoes." He wiped sweat from his neck and forehead with a rumpled handkerchief. Although it was almost sunset, there wasn't much relief from the heat. A breeze rustled the trees that screened the house from the cornfields, and the air was less humid than it was in Lincoln Prairie.

"I suppose you want to talk about that child Natalie," Harry said. "Can't tell me but what they didn't kill her."

"Do you hear from her family at all?" Vik asked.

"Ain't had nothing much to do with none of them since after the war."

"Korean War?"

"World War Two."

"Just like Cain and Abel," Opal said as she came through the screen door with a large tray and set it on an old Formica kitchen table in the far corner. The tea was served with ice and sprigs of mint.

"When their daddy died, my Harry was supposed to split the acreage with Harvey, but Harvey wasn't having none of that. He thought that because he was fifteen minutes older, he should get it all. Harvey went to court and ended up with nothing, time he got finished paying the lawyers. The will said half and half. Wasn't nothing but sixty acres on each side of this house. We've sold ours off now to the big farmers. Harvey moved to the other side of Peoria soon as the case was settled. Ain't set foot on this property since, nor we on his."

"But you know what happened to Joe's kids, Harvey's grandchildren," Vik said.

"We wanted to keep them poor little ones from the likes of him," Opal said. "Mean, that Harvey. I'm glad we've kept clear of him."

Harry reached out and patted Opal's hand. "Don't go getting your blood pressure up. We lost our son not long after he was born. There weren't no more after that. Opal here, she mothers everything. Would have been a good mother to that little Natalie, but that social worker that come here said we were too old. That Joe, he was mean, same as his daddy, same as my father, his granddaddy."

"Beatty men get mean when they get a little liquor in them. My Harry here, he don't drink nothing stronger than that tea. Good man, my Harry."

"I've got enough sense to appreciate a good woman is all."

Side by side, their rockers creaked in unison. Not a bad life, Marti thought, growing old together, content, satisfied. It seemed a shame that the only thing that mattered where Natalie was concerned was their age. She might have been happy here.

Marti took a sip of tea. "Doreen grew up in this area, too?"

191

"Dim-witted, that one," Opal said. "Had a chance to marry a decent boy and got blinded by Joe Beatty's college degree."

"She wanted to put as much distance as possible between her and her old man, most likely, and Joe didn't live here anymore," Harry said.

Opal refilled everyone's glasses. "So she married the son of his drinking buddy to do it. Dim-witted, like I said."

"Like attracts like, Opal. Joe did get her away from here."

"To what, Harry? Do you really think they lived much different than their folks? That little girl got whipped on, didn't she? Just like Harvey's kids, just like Doreen. Doreen might just as well have stayed here, for all the good it did her taking off with Joe."

"You think Joe abused Doreen?" Vik asked.

"Sure," Harry said. "Just like Harvey beat on Joe's mother, just like Doreen's father beat on her. Goes back generations."

"If she'd had a lick of sense, she wouldn't have married him," Opal said. "Shame what happened to that child."

"When you think of it," Harry said, "it wasn't really no surprise when something really bad happened to one of them."

"Too bad it ain't changed none of them for the better. Joe's brother needs to have his children taken from him before one of them gets beat to death."

"Such a pretty little thing Doreen was when she left here — blond hair, green eyes. Came back when that little girl of hers went missing, and she looked almost as old as her mother. Natalie didn't look nothing like Doreen. Some of them folks that was looking for her came around here with her picture. Natalie looked just like a Beatty. Spitting image of her daddy, she was. Never could understand how he could look at a child who looked so much like himself and then hurt her."

Instead of driving back to Lincoln Prairie, Marti and Vik called home and booked rooms in a hotel in Peoria, not far from the river. Marti turned the bed down, then sat at the desk and wrote out her notes. After three eventful but nonepic years on the force in Lincoln Prairie, she had managed to stumble across the case from hell. Not because of the time that had passed since Natalie's disappearance, or all of the people who were involved, or even the task of finding Natalie's family, but because Doreen and Joe Beatty had been born into such a tradition of abuse that by now one or both of them probably had passed those habits on to their sons.

The next morning, Vik and Marti drove back to the small town south of Peoria and had breakfast with Don Grant, the cop Vik had spoken to the day before.

"The Beattys and the Wileys, Doreen's family, farmed here for years," Grant said. He pushed long gray hair back from his forehead.

"My daddy was a cop here for thirty-five years and he got called out to their places to settle disputes. I still get calls. Calls for Joe's brother Jim, and his wife, too."

"Wife beating?" Vik said.

"Drinking, fighting, you name it."

Grant cut a biscuit with a fork, pushed it around in white gravy, and smiled as he ate it. "The old man kept a working farm until he keeled over of a heart attack and died. Once the boys got through fighting, there wasn't a lot left, but Harry kept farming for years. He made enough to keep a roof over his head and his wife happy. Like I said, a matter of pride. Harvey, on the other hand . . ." Grant munched on another mouthful of biscuit and gravy. "Harvey took what was left of his share, bought a house and half an acre, and drank up the rest. I'm not sure how his family survived. A few people looked the other way when Joe or one of the other kids stole food. Every one of them left as quick as they could, and none of them have been back, except to brag, and even that stopped after a while."

"What do you think happened to Natalie Beatty?" Vik asked.

"Well, we've all got our theories. I figure that even though Joe Beatty might have become some hotshot college-educated engineer, he hasn't ever been more than one of those mean-assed Beattys. There's not much I'd put past him, including killing that little girl. We looked three, four weeks, long after they stopped looking in McHenry. We know those folks here. It didn't seem strange to nobody that one of those Beattys would go missing one day, and it wouldn't surprise anyone if a Wiley did. That poor little Natalie was a Wiley on her momma's side and a Beatty on her daddy's. That little girl never had much of a chance."

"Do you know of anyone who's seen or heard from Joe or Doreen since Natalie went missing?"

"No, and nobody's likely to. They're not coming back here. They don't have anything left to brag about. And they don't have anyone here who would help them. Their families ain't much for taking care of their own."

Marti and Vik spent the rest of the morning going through microfiche of old newspaper clippings on the search for Natalie, as well as those on the Beattys and Wileys in general, without finding anything useful. Both the Wileys and the Beattys were in the "Police Blotter" column at least every other week.

CHAPTER 20

When Vik and Marti got back to the precinct Friday afternoon, Lupe was in court. Copies of the autopsy report on Tyrell Laws had come in, but nothing from the two agencies involved with the Beattys.

Looking at everything arranged on her desk, Marti felt overwhelmed. "I don't know what in the hell is wrong with people," she said. "They know what's going on, they know something worse is going to happen, and they do nothing but wait and then say I told you so." But Liddy Fields had done something. So had Tyrell Laws. Was that why they were dead?

Angry, she sat down and put her head in her hands. Had Joe or Doreen Beatty gone over the edge? The odds were that one of them had killed Natalie. There was nothing to suggest they couldn't kill again, although why they had waited so long was a mystery. "We need to know where in the hell they are," she said.

"We don't have a case yet," Vik said. "We can't arrest them."

Marti muttered a few profanities, liked the

sound of them, and repeated them. Then she pushed the incoming information to one side and took out a legal pad.

"So, we have one missing child and one missing family. We have no photographs of the family. Therefore, should the need or opportunity present itself, we cannot attempt to get an ID. Two people who were involved with this family are dead, both older women."

"And one homicide is outside of our jurisdiction," Vik said. "We're going to have to get a handle on the Beattys' recent whereabouts."

"They might be right under our noses," Marti said. "Or they could be in Chicago or somewhere else, which would make them a lot harder to find. There is no recent employment history for Joe or Doreen."

"We need Lupe," Vik said. "She could be checking out all of that."

It was a few minutes before six when Lupe came in. Without sitting down, she took everything out of her in basket and scanned it. "My case just went to the jury."

"You could have gone home," Marti said. "You've come in every day this week, in addition to going to court."

"I thought I'd better check to see if you needed anything."

"Better watch out," Marti said. "Sounds

like you're getting hooked. There's nothing worse than a workaholic homicide cop." Marti handed her the Beatty file, the Fields file, and what she had on Tyrell Laws.

"It's not much, but we're expecting more. Get some index cards, half a dozen different colors. Come up with a color code for each group of similar information — one item per card — and cross-reference everything. Next, type a chronology that sequentially includes the narrative on each report. Don't change a comma. Everybody sees things from a different perspective. I might miss a detail that someone else picks up on."

Marti thought for a minute. "And we need a list of names. There aren't many now, but we're waiting for two more reports. We'll need to know where everyone is — social workers, lawyers, foster parents, whoever, and, if deceased, how they died. Oh, and we need photographs of the Beattys — as recent as possible, but we'll take anything we can get."

"*Estamos bascando a una persona que está loca.* We must be looking for someone who is crazy," Lupe said, talking to herself.

When Marti said in Spanish, "*A lo mejor nosotros tendremos suerte y estaremos mal de eso.* Maybe we'll get lucky and be wrong about that," Lupe looked up, surprised that they spoke the same language.

Vik looked from Lupe to Marti. "I got *loco*,"

he said. "Is there anything else I should know?"

In Polish, Marti came as close to "We might be looking for a crazy" as she could.

Lupe looked through Marti's file. "Poor Liddy Fields," she said. "She had already worked at one school where a child was lost and later turned up dead. Then she rescues Natalie from an abusive environment, only to have her returned and then go missing. If Fields does have a daughter somewhere and we manage to find her . . . it looks like she might have lost her, too."

"Look, Torres," Vik said, "I'll tolerate an occasional interruption from you, and one or two intelligent observations even. But don't waste your markers. We still don't have anything on the sketch? How many papers did it run in?"

"Eleven statewide, including all the major cities."

"There must be a lot of those," Vik said, "in Tennessee."

"Her photo ran in six different editions." Lupe nodded toward the contents of her in basket. "I was hoping something would have come in. It will run again this weekend."

Lupe got the index cards and stacked them by color.

"Names, addresses, phone numbers, dates, places," Vik said. "Isn't that boring?"

"Boring as hell," Lupe said. She grinned. "But you two would be doing it if I wasn't, and you've got the best arrest and conviction stats in the department."

A smile twitched at the corners of Vik's mouth.

"Right now, we've got nobody to talk to and no place to start looking for the Beattys," Marti said. "Last known address was in Chicago." She took out a directory.

While Marti was working on that, Vik stuck colored pins on a wall map of the city — red for the location where Fields died and orange for Park and Central schools.

"All anyone did was try to help," he said.

"Depends on your perspective, Vik. From the looks of it, somebody might not agree."

CHAPTER 21

Marti and Vik went in to see the lieutenant first thing Saturday morning.

"So," he said after Marti explained their suspicions in the Beatty case. "What's the game plan?"

"Locate the Beattys, get the other reports, contact everyone identified in the reports, get photographs of the Beattys and show them around."

"If your suspicions are correct, what's your assessment of the perp?"

"We don't have enough information yet."

"As far as you can determine right now, is the general populace at risk?"

Marti took a deep breath. "Not as far as we can determine at this time, sir," she said. "If we're on the right track with this, the perp is interested only in anyone involved in helping Natalie escape from that abuse, and so far, our two possible victims are older women."

Upstairs, part of a DCFS report had arrived, handwritten notes by the male social worker who had quit while the case was pending. Marti read through it. "There are a few names here, people involved with the case. Maybe you should add pins to that map for whoever could possibly be at risk. Let's ignore gender and age. That might not be a legitimate factor."

Vik added four white pins to the map: Compania Ortega; Ray Olson, the psychologist who had worked with the children while they were in placement; Jamaal Hayes, the children's attorney, appointed by the court; and the foster parents, the Muldoons. Marti gave the notes to Lupe.

"See what you can add to the index cards. The copies that were faxed in are hard to read. Call Compania Ortega. Try to locate Olson and the others. Don't alarm them, but tell them to be careful. We'll follow up."

Turning to Vik, she said, "Nothing much new. These notes were written by the DCFS caseworker assigned when the Beatty children went into placement. Beatty lost his job and then went to work for another manufacturer, and they sold their house in Lincoln Prairie. This caseworker supervised one family visit, describes Natalie as shy and the boys as self-conscious. Natalie responded when her parents spoke to her but did not initiate any conversation. Natalie didn't say one word during the ride to the office where the family met. She cried all the way back to the foster home, then ran to the foster mother as soon as she got there. The caseworker says she was trembling and frightened, said she wanted to stay with the foster parents forever and pleaded with them not to make her see her parents again."

Vik and Marti drove to the Lanebrook Golf Course and met the attorney, Jamaal Hayes, on the fourth green. Jamaal was tall and muscular, with skin the color of caramel. He was with a group of four and smiled as Marti approached. After he teed off, he stood with the detectives under the tree where the golf cart was parked.

"Why Officer Mac, it's so nice to see you." Hayes was in his mid-thirties. He had what Marti's momma called bedroom eyes, and had tried to date Marti several times when she first came to Lincoln Prairie. At the time, she thought he was insensitive because he had suggested that since her husband was gone, she might need a little masculine companionship. "What's this about the Beatty case?" Hayes said. "Nobody's asked me about that in years."

"When's the last time you heard from them?" Marti asked.

"I've never heard from them. I argued vigorously that Natalie, at least, not be returned to the home. The caseworker who had just been assigned to the case disagreed. The judge ruled against me. The kids went home. What happened after that is anyone's guess."

"We don't want to alarm you," Marti said, "but we would appreciate it if you would exercise caution where the Beattys are concerned. If any member of the family contacts you, call us. Do not, under any circumstance, go near them or allow them to come near you."

Jamaal cracked his knuckles and looked toward the green. "If I ever have the good fortune to run across Joe Beatty," he said, "you will be looking for me. If I don't kill him, I will inflict considerable bodily harm."

"Be careful," Marti said.

"Oh? I don't think his type picks on adult males. The lame, the halt, the stupid, the scared, and little girls are about as much as he can manage."

"Be careful," Marti repeated, but she expected that he was right.

Jamaal shaded his eyes and watched as a ball arced somewhere beyond his line of vision. "Damn, he missed the sand bunker," he said. "Until Beatty came along, my only personal experience with child abuse and wife beating were with poor and lower-middle-class families. I didn't grow up poor, and this was something that happened in other neighborhoods, where people were hungry or using drugs and getting drunk. I honestly did not believe that garbage like

Beatty could be found where I live. Now every time I walk into a courtroom or drive down my street or meet with my broker, I ask myself, Where is he? Where's the Beatty in this crowd? Because now I know that he is there and he could be anyone."

When they got back, Lupe was taking a late lunch, the office smelled of freshly brewed coffee, and there was a box of doughnuts next to the coffeepot. Cowboy was sitting with his boots on the desk and his five-gallon hat tilted back. His blond hair was bleached almost white by the sun and his face was deeply tanned. He was leafing through a stack of girlie magazines.

"Research?" Marti asked. As soon as she sat down, Slim sauntered over and gave her a dimpled smile.

"Sure is nice to have you around here without your partner, Miss Marti."

"Partner? Vik's right there."

"I was talking about our little Latin spit-fire. Torres just doesn't have the personality to be a detective. She's strictly a street cop."

"You two having a little trouble taming her?"

Slim shook his head. "I knew you'd been around long enough to understand. We've got five people in one little office."

"And two of them are women. Are you beginning to feel like you're outnumbered?"

"Me and Cowboy prefer our women to

have experience, finesse, expertise."

"Yes," Marti agreed. "I can understand that. Men with your . . . background must be very selective."

Slim gave her another slow, easy smile.

"In fact, Slim, it really surprises me that with all you two know about women you seem to be having so much difficulty with Lupe."

"It's a mystery to me, too," Slim agreed.

"May I make a suggestion?"

"That's what I was hoping you'd say."

"Sometimes a woman wants a relationship that's based on mutual respect. Maybe if you tried pretending to be mature. Adult behavior can be a real turn-on."

Cowboy slapped down a magazine. "Gotcha! Score one for Big Mac."

"And Cowboy," Marti said, "if you want to impress Lupe with your intellectual prowess, you might want to try something a little less infantile, too. Maybe an intelligent discussion on how she handles those gang-bangers and drug dealers she locks up when she's not volunteering to put up with Curly and Moe to help Vik and me."

"Score two for Big Mac," Vik said without humor. "And she's right about those magazines. You've got two female cops on your hands here. You'd better get a grip before you lose it. It's no wonder you're both still single. I don't think there's a woman out there stupid enough to put up with you."

With great effort, Marti kept her mouth from dropping open. When Lupe came in, the magazines were gone, and not long after, Slim and Cowboy were out the door.

"I don't have much," Lupe said. "Joe Beatty was terminated at the plant he was working at when the children were taken. He got a similar management position at a manufacturing plant in McHenry, then was terminated when Natalie went missing. It was all downhill after that. He had a job as a foreman, then one on an assembly line. He got fired for drinking on the job. Then the jobs dried up and he went on unemployment. There's no record of any other employment or any type of assistance when his unemployment benefits ran out. His last known address, while he was collecting unemployment, was an SRO in Chicago. Doreen and both boys lived with him."

"Maybe they went from the SRO to the streets," Marti said.

"They never made any contact with public aid for assistance," Lupe said. "No medical card, food stamps, nothing."

"Makes sense," Vik said. "DCFS was the cause of it all. Did you talk with Compania Ortega?"

"Not yet," Lupe said. "I left messages on her machines at work and at home that she not have contact with any of the Beattys and that she call us at her earliest conven- ience."

"Maybe order of intervention is a pattern," Marti said.

"Who knows," Vik said. "Maybe we have two perps and two unrelated homicides. About the only luck we're having with this so far is a short list of potential victims, if our assumptions are correct."

"We've got some real loose threads here," Marti cautioned. "Our whole theory could unravel in the next five minutes."

Trust your instincts, Johnny would have said. Her instincts told her they were going in the right direction.

"We need photographs," she said. "If the family is on the streets, we might find a trail, shelters or soup kitchens, something."

"There's nothing on them for two years," Lupe said. "I bet they really aren't around here."

"Keep thinking like that," Vik said, "and you're going back to gangs and drugs. Pat- terns," he said. "Perps are predictable once you figure them out, and most of them are stupid. Joe Beatty didn't even go out of state when he went to college. He only went as far as Peoria to show off. Not much chance he'll take off for unfamiliar sur- roundings just because he killed a few people. He's going to stick real close to what he knows. He might be right here in Lincoln

Prairie. We might not know a hell of a lot right now, but habits do win out."

"Then we might need habits to find him. People at shelters don't like to talk," Lupe said. "Clients don't always give their right names unless they have to. And we don't have current descriptions."

"A realist," Vik said. "Look, kid, homicide cases are the stuff nightmares are made of. Don't limit your possibilities by assuming your perp thinks smart. Who's to say Beatty's not using his own name, and throwing it around at that? He knows he's too smart to get caught, because he's still out there. That's the best thing we've got going for us right now."

Marti put in another call to the agencies that still hadn't sent reports. Everyone promised expediency. "Expedient was yesterday," Marti told them. "We need the information now."

It was almost dusk when Compania Ortega pulled into her driveway. She used the remote to open the garage door, then drove in and closed the door behind her. She had spent most of the day shopping. She pushed the button that popped open the trunk and got out. A noise startled her and she turned in the direction of the sound.

CHAPTER 22

It was getting dark when Marti and Vik pulled up near Compania Ortega's house. An ambulance was parked in front, flanked by four squads with lights flashing. Dr. Cyprian's car was parked across the street. Yellow tape marked off the driveway and the garage. Floodlights were set up. A crowd had gathered on the other side of the barricades, about forty people, Marti estimated. They were restive but quiet. Four carnations and a rose had been placed on the front steps.

Marti took her camera out of the trunk. While Vik located the first cop on the scene, Marti went to the entrance of the garage. An evidence tech motioned to her to keep out. From where she stood, she could see broken crockery and ceramics all over the place. Someone must have heard it being smashed.

Dr. Cyprian stood up. "Multiple trauma to the head," he said. "And glass embedded in the scalp. She has a kiln over in the far corner. I'm certain she was struck with several of whatever these were, but she was killed first, with that mold."

The mold looked like it was made of marble. "Anything else?" Marti asked.

"She struck out at her attacker, but there was no real fight. We've got something under the fingernails, though. The first blow was very forceful. I would also guess that the first missed her. See the dent in the car?"

Half of the rear fender was caved in.

When the evidence techs were finished, Marti stopped one of them. "I need everything you've got as fast as you can give it to me." She went over to look at the body. The only thing recognizable above the neck was Ortega's long black hair. For a moment, she felt a terrible sadness. Compania Ortega had given Natalie Beatty her own toys to play with and a year without violence. How many other children had she helped? How could that have anything to do with why she was dead? Standing up, Marti began taking pictures.

"We'd better move fast on this one," she said when Vik came in. "If it has anything to do with the Beattys, it looks like someone's losing control."

Ortega's fiancé, a short, stocky man with a sideburns and a mustache, had found the body. He was sitting in the back of a squad car, weeping quietly.

"Sir, could you answer just a few questions?" Vik asked.

The man nodded.

Marti gave Vik a handful of Kleenex and Vik pressed them into the man's hand. "You were engaged to Miss Ortega?"

"Yes, I'm Ricardo, her fiancé."

"And when's the last time you saw her, Ricardo, before you arrived here?"

The man blew his nose. "Last night. Tonight we were going to fix dinner and then go to a late movie."

"Did she seem okay?"

"She said she must be very careful, that maybe she would need some kind of alarm system and that we would have to talk about it."

"What did you think might be wrong?"

"There had been some threat about a week ago, a man who was accused of molesting the children. The mother was angry because he was put in jail and the children removed. I thought that must be what this was about, although there have been threats before."

"What time did you find her, sir?"

"About seven o'clock. She was . . . she was . . ." He put his hands to his face and began sobbing.

Vik got the name of the couple Ricardo had referred to from Ortega's supervisor and ordered them picked up immediately.

By 10:30, they had questioned the man, who was out on bail, and the woman and verified their alibis. It took another two and a half hours to canvass every house in a two-block radius. Uniforms canvassed farther out.

One man, walking his dog after dinner, had noticed an old Chevy that he had never seen in the neighborhood before. It was maroon and rusty, with a trunk lid that didn't quite match the rest of the paint job, and was parked a block and half west of Ortega's house. Another man described the same car driving slowly down the street around 3:30 that afternoon. A woman who lived two houses east of Ortega had seen a thin man wearing old jeans walk past about four o'clock. Nobody had seen anyone approach or enter the garage. Nobody had observed anyone leaving. Close to seven, a kid had gone past the place where the man saw the Chevy. The car was gone.

"Good neighbors," Vik said as they headed to the precinct. "We've got a lot of information. And we can narrow down the time."

Ten minutes later, they were talking with two teenagers who had found a bloody shirt four blocks from the crime scene. A uniform found bloody tennis shoes along the side of the road about six blocks away.

"Feast or famine," Vik said.

"Feast is better, Jessenovik. Cyprian says

we've even got some scrapings under her fingernails. This is almost like winning the lottery."

"Not until we can match some of this to the perp and get a positive ID."

At midnight, they got a call from the lab. "We've got a match on some soil samples."

"Dirt?" Marti said.

"Right. We found some dirt in Ortega's garage, found the same dirt in the treads of the tennis shoes. We also found a footprint that matches up with the tennis shoe. By morning, we'll be able to give you some idea of height and weight."

Marti was effusive in her praise.

"Dirt," she told Vik when she hung up. "Dirt."

"Big deal. We found dirt at Sophia Admunds's place, too. Too bad it didn't match anything near Warren's house. And no confession yet."

"Dirt, Vik."

"Right. I know."

"And we found dirt at the Admunds place."

"Marti, we're not breaking new ground here."

She called the lab and got the answering machine. The staff was gone for the night. At the beep, she said, "Compare the dirt you found in Ortega's garage with what you found at the Admunds place."

"MacAlister. We'll be a laughingstock," Vik said.

"It's probably nothing," Marti agreed. "But it isn't that often that we get two cases within such a short span of time where dirt is this important. What the hell."

Marti wrote up her notes before going home. She fell into bed at a quarter to four.

CHAPTER 23

Marti was awakened by her beeper. She hadn't heard the alarm go off.

"Coming to work today?" Vik sounded as sleepy as she felt, and as cranky.

"Where are you?" she asked.

"I went to the Ortega autopsy. I just made it in. Where are you?"

"Still in bed." Her eyes didn't want to stay open. "What time is it?"

"Ten to eight." She had slept through roll call. Sharon and the kids must have assumed she'd already left for work.

"I'll be there in forty-five minutes."

It took her thirty-five minutes to shower, dress, and drive to work. When she arrived at her desk, she found additional DCFS files on the Beattys that had been faxed to the wrong department.

"No new information," Marti said after she read through the typed and dated notes. "Just everything you never wanted to know and hoped to God nobody would ever tell you about ways to abuse a child without breaking any bones or leaving marks. This is from an interim caseworker. After the

216

visit with her parents, Natalie told her foster mother what they had done."

Hours of standing on tiptoe in a corner or kneeling in a dark closet; cold baths; a mat on the floor in the cellar, where she slept naked, without a blanket; being made to drink liquid detergent. Mean, spiteful things, Marti thought.

To her surprise, Vik reached out for the report. He was quiet for a long time after he read through it. "We're going to find this bastard, and find out what happened to Natalie. Nobody should get away with this," he said.

Marti read through the *News-Times* as well as the *Chicago Tribune*'s versions of Ortega's death. She had asked the *News-Times* not to sensationalize it, and although the article was on the front page, it was brief. The only photo was of the crowd in front of Ortega's house, and that was on page six. The *Tribune* ran a two-inch column on the bottom of page four in section two. The level of exposure in the Fields and the Laws cases was limited, as well. If they were dealing with one perp, Marti didn't want to step up the level of visibility. Perps who were multiple killers often fed on the publicity. She showed the *Trib* article to Vik.

"If the killer was expecting a lot of attention, I hope he was disappointed."

"Right. Maybe he'll get so frustrated that he'll call the police and turn himself in." He reached for the *News-Times*. "And maybe a certain psychic who has dreams won't bother to come in."

Marti had all but forgotten about Alma Miller.

"Excuse me," Lupe said. "Sorry to interrupt. I've confirmed that Ray Olson, the psychologist, is on vacation, but I can't get in touch with the foster parents. Is it okay if I have a unit sent over to check things out?"

"Good idea, Torres," Vik said. "And, Marti, we need to canvass Ortega's neighborhood again and see if anyone else saw the man in the old maroon car or the man walking near Ortega's house. Unfortunately, the people who came in this morning to give descriptions for a composite of the Beattys didn't give the artist enough to develop anything we can use."

The canvass produced one more sighting of a man walking down the street. This woman thought he was older because of his glasses. They went through Ortega's personal effects again. The wedding invitations were ready to be sent out and a lacy white dress with a matching mantilla was in a plastic bag in a closet. There was nothing to indicate why anyone would kill her.

"Well," Vik said, "that leaves us to the

main task at hand, finding the needles in the haystack."

"The Beattys — the reports aren't telling us enough about them, Vik, and the people we've talked to don't know enough, either. Where would they hide? What's familiar to them? What do they care about? Where do they feel safe?" She massaged the back of her neck. "And who's they? Are they all still together?"

Vik walked over to the map they had dotted with color-coded pushpins. "And where in the hell would they go?" He consulted Lupe's notes and added black and yellow pins. "Where they lived and where Joe worked in Lake County." He stood away from the map, then checked something up close, consulted the notes again, and went to the phone.

"The place that Joe built was vandalized the weekend before the Fourth," he said when he hung up. "Realtor says he went over to check it on Friday the twenty-eighth and everything was okay, went back with the client on Monday and it was a mess. And it's closer to where Admunds used to live than I thought — about a block over."

"Is there much vandalism in that neighborhood?" Marti asked.

"This is an all-time first. The mayor lives on the next block."

"Maybe we should check it out."

"The Realtor's going to meet us there."

The house Joe Beatty had built was white brick with black trim and few windows. A shoulder-high white brick fence protected it from view. It was different from the more conservative Victorians and Tudors in the neighborhood, and conspicuous because the lot had no trees. Marti had driven past it several times. Theo called it "the fortress."

"Isolated somehow, isn't it?" Vik said. "Sterile."

"I wouldn't feel encouraged to drop in," Marti agreed.

"The Realtor said it's been empty two years and they foreclosed on the last owner when he couldn't find anyone who wanted to buy it."

"It is a nice house. It just doesn't belong here. If it were in Barrington, or Lincoln-shire maybe, it probably would sell as soon as it went on the market."

She wondered why Beatty chose Lincoln Prairie. It wasn't near where he worked, nor was it likely to endear him to his neighbors. Maybe he wanted to be left alone.

The real estate agent pulled up and got out of his car. The house was dark inside. The front of the house was like a narrow hallway. The rooms that opened off of it had no windows at all.

"The place has an alarm system," the

Realtor said. "But we never bothered turning it on, not in this neighborhood. Besides, there nothing here to take but the light fixtures, plumbing, things like that."

The first room they went into had the carpet ripped up and holes punched or kicked into the walls. Wiring and light fixtures had been ripped out.

"Living room," the agent said.

"What does the claims adjuster think caused the damage?" Vik asked.

"A human hand or foot."

"Everything?" Marti said.

"Yes. It has something to do with the patterns or the shapes of the holes. Someone from your police department came out, too. It sounds scientific when they explain it. I told them I thought it was someone who had a grudge against the last owner and couldn't find him to get even."

All of the other rooms were in the same condition.

"Looks like whoever did it was mad as hell," Vik said when they went outside.

"That's my guess," Marti agreed. But did it have anything at all to do with the Beattys? They hadn't lived there in years.

They drove around the block and found the Victorian where the Admundses once lived. Their property abutted the Beattys'. The brick fence would have kept Sophia from seeing much, at least from the first floor.

"I wonder how much she could see from upstairs," Marti said.

"She could see into the yard. I think the way the roof over hangs would have kept her from seeing anything else."

They decided to see if there were any surprises at the place the Beattys bought in McHenry.

"Gives us a chance to see where the girl went missing, too," Vik said.

Marti wasn't sure she wanted to know.

Marti and Vik drove out to McHenry and stopped by the Realtor's to pick up the keys to the house where the Beattys had lived. It was a short dead-end street, quiet except for the drone of lawn mowers. Sprinklers watered the grass. Birds chattered. The Beatty house was a sprawling ranch with blue siding and white trim and a FOR SALE sign in front. A weathered six-foot-high fence enclosed most of the yard. According to the Realtor, ownership had changed four times since the Beattys filed for bankruptcy and the mortgage company foreclosed. Marti unlocked the front door. A window had been broken. They entered with guns drawn. Each room and every closet was clean, empty, and uninhabited, until they checked the basement. They stopped mid-way down the stairs.

The one large unfinished room had a sink,

washer, and dryer lined up along one wall and floor-to-ceiling shelves on another. The floor was littered with beer cans, pop cans, and fast-food bags and wrappers. A pile of clothes lay in one corner. Without disturbing anything, they made sure nobody was inside or under the clothing, then called the local police force.

It took the local cops about an hour to go through the place. Other than confirming that someone had indeed broken in and apparently lived there, they didn't come up with much. When Vik requested soil samples within a two-block radius, the evidence tech started to say something, then shrugged and agreed.

Marti and Vik went to the room identified on the McHenry report as the one Natalie had been sleeping in the night she disappeared. Natalie could not have gone out the window without assistance. The drop to the ground was at least twelve feet. If her parents' bedroom was the second one down the hall, they might not have heard someone entering if Natalie hadn't given any alarm. But anyone outside would need a ladder to get in. And since there was no gate and the only way to access the yard from the house was through the kitchen door, someone would have had to help Natalie over the fence, or taken her out the front door.

"We're too late," Vik said. "Whoever was

staying here could have been here last night."

"Or last week, or last month, Jessenovik."

Vik hit the palm of his hand with his fist. "We could have just missed them."

"Maybe they'll be back."

"The local force will keep their eyes on the place, but . . ."

"They'd love to catch whoever was in here. It could be part of a homicide investigation. They'll do a real good job of watching this place and catching anyone who looks suspicious."

"If we'd thought of this sooner, we might have caught them."

"Oh come on, Jessenovik. We might not have much to go on, but look at it this way: If any member of the Beatty family was living here, this means that we've at least started to figure out how they think."

The Beattys' last known address before they moved to the SRO in Chicago was on the south side of Lincoln Prairie in an area that was now predominantly Hispanic. It had been a rental unit when the Beattys lived there. The chipped and peeling paint on the small wood-frame bungalow had been painted over recently — salmon pink with mint green trim. Tall yellow sunflowers grew on one side of the house and dahlias and daylilies on the other. The sky was such a clear blue and the grass such a deep green that Marti thought of Tahitian scenes painted by Gauguin. The white brick house that Theo called the fortress seemed more than just a few neighborhoods and a couple dozen city blocks away. An older couple opened the door. They had bought the house from a cousin and the name Beatty meant nothing.

"Well," Vik said, "whatever happened to Natalie, nothing good happened to her family once she was gone."

They had come up empty again. Who had been living in the house in McHenry? Where were the Beattys now? Something nagged at Marti for a minute, but she was too tired to figure out what it was.

CHAPTER 24

A package from the attorney, Jamaal Hayes, had been delivered while they were out. "Copies of his files," Marti said. "And we've got pictures — school photographs — Natalie at seven, Max at nine, and Vaughn at eleven." How much had they changed?

Both boys had dark hair and brown eyes like Natalie's, and neither smiled. They had unremarkable faces with ordinary features that might not have changed much over time. Inconspicuous was a good way to describe them. Few people were likely to take a second look or remember if they saw them. Marti covered their mouths and looked at their eyes. They didn't seem happy or sad, just — what? — disinterested, detached . . . both of them. There were no photographs of their parents, Doreen and Joe.

Marti leaned back for a minute and squeezed her eyes shut. She felt so tired that she was afraid she was missing something. The clues they had were so meager that if she did miss anything significant, it could mean blowing the whole case.

"Hungry?" Vik asked.

"No. Just tired." She began thumbing through Jamaal's notes.

"Look, Marti, let's give these photos to the artist and let him age the kids a bit. Then we can call it a day. If we come to it fresh after a decent night's sleep, who knows? Hell, maybe Joe Beatty's a psychopath who killed off the whole family and is working his way through his enemies."

"Let's just try to keep a grasp on reality," Marti said, but it didn't seem like an implausible theory. Was there a time when she would have found Vik's scenario unthinkable? She took the police-file photo of Natalie out of the envelope and put it with Jamaal's. Natalie was smiling in the school picture — taken while she was in foster care — even though the smile was tentative. There was a wistfulness in her eyes. In Jamaal's photo — taken while she was still living at home — there was no smile and her eyes seemed empty.

Marti lined up Natalie's picture with those of her brothers. Were all of them dead? Every time a child was involved, all she could think of was something that her momma always said — that they didn't ask to come here. It seemed a malicious kind of cruelty to give someone life, only to inflict pain. Instead of putting the photographs away, Marti left them near the top of her desk. Whether victim or witness, terrible things had happened to them when they were young and vulnerable. Someone needed to remember that. She needed to remember that. If somebody was killing off the few advocates these children had, they would have to be stopped.

Marti passed everything to Vik. There were bags under his eyes.

"You look tired, Jessenovik."

"Have you checked the mirror today?" He ran his fingers through his hair.

"Stop or you'll have it standing on end."

"Hey, guys," Lupe interrupted. "We've found the foster parents. Mrs. Muldoon is in intensive care at Lincoln Prairie General. She was mugged in a parking lot at a mall last night. Her husband is at the hospital, too."

Mr. Muldoon was four inches taller than Vik's six two and twenty pounds heavier. He was ruddy-faced and gave the impression of athleticism. Marti thought something about him was familiar.

"Madman Muldoon," Vik said, extending his hand.

Marti looked from one of them to the other.

"The wrestler," Vik said, and introduced her.

"Retired," Muldoon said.

He looked close to fifty.

Marti braced herself when he shook her hand, but his grip wasn't tight. It was difficult to think of a professional wrestler as a foster parent.

"How's your wife?" Vik asked.

"If I find the bastard who did this, he's dead."

"Can she talk to us?"

"Man, she's unconscious. They had to operate to relieve the pressure on her brain. They've got her breathing on her own, though. The doctor says that's a good sign. He's not taking any bets on whether she'll wake up."

Muldoon turned away and walked to the window. "I've been with that woman close to thirty years now."

"You haven't by any chance heard from any of the Beattys, have you?" Vik asked.

"Natalie . . ." His eyes narrowed. "No. Why?"

"We're looking for them."

"Which one?"

"Anyone we can find."

"Because of Natalie?"

"Yes," Vik lied.

"No. The social worker came and got them. Six weeks later, little Nat was gone. She used to get up in the morning and fix my toast for me. We both liked it a little burned, with pineapple jam. We'd sit in the kitchen and watch the horses from the window until my wife got up. That was our time — just me and Nat. It only took me a couple of months to get her to go out to the barn. She wouldn't ride until spring."

Muldoon was silent and neither Vik nor Marti spoke until he cleared his throat and turned toward them.

"What do you think happened to her?" Vik asked.

"I think she's dead. And if you're looking for Joe Beatty, you'd better find him first. I know how to hurt him real bad. At least as bad as he hurt Nat, and for a long time without killing him."

"Do you have any idea of where the boys could be? They've both dropped out of school."

Muldoon thought about that. "Vaughn, he's a loner. He'd keep to himself. But Max, he was a lot like Nat, as hard as he tried not to be. He'd want to be around people — a gang, a crowd, anything. You'd have to be looking for him to notice him, though. He was real good at not calling any attention to himself."

He checked his watch. "I can see her again."

Vik looked at Marti, then looked toward the door. She nodded. It seemed like a good time to leave.

On their way back to the precinct, they got a call that Jamaal Hayes was waiting to see them. When they got back to the precinct, he was there.

"Composites," he said, handing them a manila folder. "I sat down with your artist. He got the Beattys real good the way they looked seven years ago, then played around with aging and hard living for a while."

Marti looked at the folder for a long minute, then opened it. Joe had the same ordinary features as his sons. And Harry Beatty had been right: Natalie looked just like a Beatty. There was something about Doreen that Marti couldn't quite figure out. Her blond hair was shoulder-length and straight, with long bangs that touched arched eyebrows. Full lips gave her a pouty sensuality. But there was a vacant expression in her eyes. "It's almost as if she's not really there."

"Spacey," Jamaal agreed. "You could be talking to her and she'd just space out, wouldn't hear you anymore, wouldn't be there."

Marti's eyes were beginning to burn. She squeezed them shut, then began blinking rapidly. "Long day," she said.

"And it's late and I'm not going to keep you," Jamaal said. "Look, I thought there might be some way I could help."

231

"Find the Beattys for us."

"Seriously?"

She explained about their difficulty in locating them.

"Why do you want to find them?"

"We just need to ask them some questions."

Jamaal smiled. "She says that in cop talk and with a straight face."

Marti shrugged. "Think of it as client privilege."

"Touché, Officer Mac." He pointed his finger at her as if it was the muzzle of a gun. "Maybe I can help. I do some pro bono work for the food pantry and the shelter program. Everyone is protective of the clients, but maybe, given the circumstances, someone would look at a composite and talk."

As Marti walked to the parking lot with Vik and Jamaal, she hoped she could stay awake long enough to drive home without having an accident.

CHAPTER 25

When Marti got home, everyone was in the den watching a movie — Sharon and Lisa, Ben and Mike, Theo and Joanna. There was a bowl of popcorn on the table and what was left of a chocolate cake with yellow icing that looked like sunflower petals.

Marti stared at the cake. It was July twenty-first, Ben's fortieth birthday, and she had forgotten. "I got you a card," she said, "but I can't remember what I did with it. And your present, it's still at the jeweler's." Tears came to her eyes. "I'm so sorry."

"It's okay, Ma," Theo said. "Me and Mike gave Ben a real chef's hat and apron and Joanna baked this cake. It's not carob, either. She used real cake mix."

Marti rubbed his short cap of kinky hair. "I forgot," she said. "I was late for your birthday; I got called out on a case half an hour before Joanna's birthday party, and now this." She collapsed on the sofa and kicked off her shoes.

Ben came over and sat beside her. "You

233

look exhausted," he said. "Have you had anything to eat lately?"

Marti couldn't remember. She shook her head.

"You work too hard, Ma," Theo said. "I'll fix you a surprise."

While he was gone, Ben said, "He's been kind of quiet, and he kept insisting that we wait because you wouldn't forget and you were coming. I thought maybe if he stayed up until you got home and got a chance to see you, he'd feel better. Don't get the guilts. We talked about it. He understands. He just missed you."

Marti did feel guilty. She went to the kitchen. Theo was making her two grilled cheese sandwiches. There was a glass of iced tea on a tray.

"Can I have the tea now?"

"Sure, there's lots. Joanna just made it."

She drained the glass and poured more. "I've been away a lot this week. I'm away a lot most of the time. And now I missed Ben's party."

Theo checked the sandwiches and flipped them. "I'm getting pretty good at this. Wait until you taste them. Two kinds of cheese — real cheese. And sliced tomatoes from my garden."

"You're upset."

Theo turned off the heat and put the sandwiches on a plate.

"Talk to me," Marti said. She was too tired

to try to coax him into it.

"You know I'd like it if you were home more, Ma. But I like it when you find out who killed people, too. Ben says I can't have it both ways. And when you're not on a case, you do spend a lot of time with us. I guess I'd like something like — a special time, like having a schedule, just the two of us."

Marti could not believe Theo was talking to her and telling her something important.

"Have you been having talks with Ben lately?"

"Oh, we have men talks a lot. Ben's cool. He's not my dad, but he's cool."

"I'm going to think about this, Theo. But if I figure out when we can have a special time, we're going to have to make a deal. I won't be a no-show unless I absolutely have to, and you won't get too upset when that happens. Now let me work out the details, okay?"

"Deal." Theo carried the tray with the sandwiches to the family room.

Later, when everyone else was in bed, Marti told Ben what had happened in the kitchen.

"This is the first time Theo has ever talked to me like that. I couldn't believe it. There is no way that we aren't going to have a special time together as often as I can manage it. What a neat idea. Cool," she amended. "What else have you two been up to?"

Ben put his arm around her shoulders and pulled her against his chest. "It isn't easy, you know, trying to figure you out, trying to understand where I fit, how I fit — even if I fit — in your life. Yours is not the typical occupation."

She had no idea what it would be like if she had three people at home waiting for her, and one of them a new husband. Ben was a paramedic, not another cop. "And?"

"Well, one thing is the kids. They're growing up. They're not ready to be on their own, but they're getting too old for baby-sitters. And they miss you when you're not around much. Then you get the guilts, and then you get grouchy. So, here we are one day, all together and all of this is going on and nobody is happy. I thought maybe we could start working out some of it now. Theo and Joanna have a real appreciation for your work. They just want a cop in the family and a mother, too."

"It's your birthday. What if I hadn't come home?"

"We had a contingency plan. Joanna was going to bake another cake tomorrow and we were going to have another party. In fact, it sounded like such a good idea that I think she's going to bake again anyway."

Marti yawned. She stopped trying to keep

her eyes open and nestled against Ben. "Ummm."

"You can wake them up when you come home, Marti."

"School. They'd be tired."

"They're kids. They'd go right back to sleep."

Maybe that wasn't such a bad idea. It would probably beat the hell out of feeling bad when she missed seeing them before they went to bed.

Ben shook her awake. "I need my shoulder back. I've got to go to work."

Marti walked him to the door and promised to go right to bed. She made it as far as the living room and lay down — just for a minute, she told herself — on the sofa.

CHAPTER 26

By three o'clock Monday afternoon, Marti and Vik were driving through the grounds of the state mental hospital in Elgin. Two-story redbrick buildings were surrounded by spacious lawns. Some were shaded by trees. Many had been empty for years. Heavy wire screens secured the windows.

"They can call this a hospital if they want to," Vik said.

"Just another kind of prison," Marti agreed. She turned off the air conditioning and opened the car windows. They had stopped for lunch at a Burger King and the car smelled of the Whoppers and fries in a bag on the backseat.

"And the bad news is that we turned over every rock out there and only managed to come up with one Beatty."

Along with Lupe, they had spent the morning exhausting every source they could think of trying to locate the Beattys. Doreen Beatty had been involuntarily committed to this hospital nine days ago after a suicide attempt. Lupe hit the magic combination. Doreen was using her maiden name, Wiley. She had been taken to a hospital in Chicago before being committed to a state facility.

Marti identified the building she was looking for by the cars parked outside. They were admitted to the forensic unit on the first floor and taken to a small office. The sun was shining through the metal screens and made diamond-shaped patterns on the brown tile floor. Marti looked at the heavy frames bolted to the brick and shivered.

"Don't get twitchy," Vik said.

She rubbed her arms, suddenly chilled. "God, I hate places like this."

The door opened.

"Here we are," a nurse said.

Marti turned to see an emaciated woman shuffle in, and she tried not to appear shocked by Doreen's appearance. The woman was wearing a pair of baggy cotton slacks and a blouse that fit tightly across her bloated stomach. Her blond hair looked like someone had taken a pair of pinking shears to it. She was shaved bald in spots. There were small round scars on her arms that looked like cigarette burns. Her pouty smile was gone forever. There was a scar on her lip and that side of her mouth sagged. She was only thirty-seven. The nurse held her elbow, guided her to the table in the center of the room, and helped her to sit down.

"What's she taking?" Marti asked.

"Stelazine and Cogentin."

Doreen sat still and looked down at the scarred table. She would have really been zombied out if she'd been on Thorazine. With Stelazine, Marti thought she might be able to get her to talk. Vik went to the window and stood with his back to them.

Nobody had checked the bag of food. Marti put it on the table and sat down. "Would you like something to eat, Doreen?" She unwrapped the burgers, took out the fries and cherry pie, and pushed a straw through the lid for the milk shake.

Without looking up, Doreen encircled the food and pulled everything toward her with arms so thin, her veins showed blue. She ate without pausing until everything was gone.

"I hear the food is pretty bad in here," Marti said.

Doreen wrapped her arms about herself and began rocking as she looked down at the table.

"I'm trying to find your children."

No response.

"Or your husband."

Doreen twisted around in the chair and looked at the door. She didn't attempt to get up.

"How are your children, Doreen?"

She shook her head.

"Do they know you're here? Does Joe know?"

"No." She spoke in a raspy whisper. "Don't tell them, okay?" Her speech was clear but slow, her voice flat.

"Why don't you want them to know?"

"They might come and get me."

"Would you rather be here?"

Doreen nodded.

"Then maybe I won't say a word to anyone. This is our secret. I thought maybe they could help me find Natalie."

Doreen looked up. Her faded blue eyes were almost alert. "My baby."

"Yes," Marti said. "Your baby."

"She was always such a good little girl." Doreen folded her arms and began to bang her head on the table.

"No, Doreen. Don't hurt yourself. It's all right. Everything is all right. You're safe here."

The banging stopped, but Marti suspected it was only because she insisted.

"Is Natalie safe?" Marti asked.

Without looking up, Doreen reached out and squeezed Marti's arm. "She was a good girl. No matter what they tell you, don't believe them. She never did anything bad."

"Do you know where she is?"

Doreen shook her head. "I couldn't help her. They took her away."

"Why?"

"Because she was good."

"Who took her?"

"They wouldn't tell me." She sounded so sad that Marti believed her.

"Do you know where they are?"

"No!" She became alarmed. "Please don't tell them I'm here."

"I promise," Marti said. "I won't tell."

Calmer, Doreen said, "I ran away from them."

"When?"

"I don't know."

"Was it hot?"

"No. Snow. It was cold. Snow. Cold. Snow." Doreen smiled, as if remembering, then stared at a place on the wall. At one point, she smiled, but she didn't respond to anything else Marti said. It was as if she wasn't there anymore. Marti recalled what Jamaal had said about Doreen spacing out, and she wondered what she was thinking of that took her mind so far away from her body.

They spoke with the doctor on the way out. "She will be here for a very long while," he said. "When there is no one to beat or abuse her, she self-mutilates."

"That poor woman's in another box," Vik said as they pulled out of the parking lot. "That monstrosity of a house Joe Beatty built was just a lot more expensive. This place is better in a way. It's got more windows."

"A box," Marti said. "He must have designed it that way on purpose, so nobody could see in." And so nobody could see out, she thought. What was it that Alma Miller had dreamed of? A big empty house without windows. A box. "All of those lovely old homes in that area and Beatty built that. The neighbors must have been furious."

"I bet it ticked off Sophia Admunds."

"Why?"

"That lot was just a big yard with trees until the people who owned it parceled it off. Big change if your property abuts it."

"I suppose." Marti thought for a minute. "I wonder what Sophia saw."

"What could she see? You were there."

"I know. The house was so isolated, and those windows were so high and so small, and that overhanging roof. But there's also what she could have heard from other neighbors."

"Marti, Admunds's husband was sick. She must have been upset about having to move. I don't think she had much time for the Beattys."

They drove for a few blocks. "When we get back, let's drop in on Warren unannounced," Vik said.

It was almost eight o'clock when they

arrived in Gurnee to see the Admundses.

Warren's house was a brick peaked-roofed quad level with five garages. It was built on a lot with a mature stand of silver birches and red maples. Everyone was on the patio. The mosquito population was at an all-time high. Citronella candles burned as bug lamps buzzed and crackled. Warren's wife was floating on her back in an oval-shaped in-ground pool. A white bikini bra hung over the back of a chair and Marti could see that Mrs. Admunds was wearing the bottom.

Warren and Jori were wearing shorts and T-shirts.

"So, what is this all about?" Jori asked.

Marti wondered if Warren had explained about his mother's money yet and if the family had discussed Gilbert's investments from the sale of the jewels.

"Does the name Beatty mean anything to you?" Vik asked.

Warren shrugged.

"Do you remember that white brick house right behind yours?"

"That monstrosity?" Warren said. "That was the worse display of bad taste that I've ever seen in my life. Were the Beattys the owners?"

"Yes," Marti said. "And they had children."

"That little girl," Jori said. "Mother insisted that they were really mean to her.

She said she saw the father in the yard one day making the child eat dirt. I thought she was just stressed out with Daddy being sick and all, but she went ahead and called the authorities."

"I hope she didn't cause them any trouble," Warren said. "My sister Nadya —"

Jori silenced him with a look. "When Dad got really sick and they had to move and then Dad died and Mother continued to worry about the child, Nadya said it was displaced grief. She said Ma was reverting to what she was most familiar with, caring for children, but that now there were none, except for that little girl."

Warren made himself a drink.

"That little girl disappeared seven years ago," Marti said. "She's never been found."

"Dear Lord," Jori said. "I had no idea. Does that mean Mother was right?"

"See," Warren said. "What did Nadya tell you?"

"That everything was in mother's mind! Do you mean to tell me that all that time, while we were humoring her, Mother was worrying about something that was real?"

"It looks that way, ma'am," Vik said.

"My God," Jori said. "All those years when we thought she was getting mean and crabby, she was probably just upset because she couldn't help that little girl. Remember how she kept telling Nadya how lucky her children were and how little they appreciated it?"

"Jori, come on," Warren said. "You always have to get so dramatic."

"Me dramatic? No matter what you say now, Warren, she was always a good mother." Jori's voice rose. "She wouldn't give you the money because she knew you didn't have the common sense of a flea. You were always the lazy one, Warren, always expecting things to come easy. That's why she wouldn't give you the money. So what did you do, you selfish slob? You took it! And there she was, all that time worrying about that little girl while you, Warren, were being inconsiderate and selfish." She turned away from him. "I cannot believe that you could live right here and have no idea what was going on, what happened to that child, why mother was so irritable and depressed. I just can't believe that after years of sacrifice the only thanks you could think of was to steal her inheritance."

Warren gulped down his drink. "Talking about me now, Jori, or yourself? You didn't hang around once you got your degree."

"Ma'am," Vik interrupted. "Sir. Do either of you recognize any of these sketches?"

Neither of them did. Nor did they recognize Natalie's school photo.

"It's a damned good thing we didn't arrest

246

Warren," Vik said as they walked to the car. "Even though someone should lock him up. He could give people dumb lessons." He loosened his tie. "Sophia Admunds probably was upset, and not just about Natalie. She was expecting a real-estate agent."

"And she could have gotten careless about who she let in." Marti thought for a minute. "She said something to Neda Wagner about whoever it was." As she turned the key in the ignition, she remembered. "Something about the young having no respect. He must have come to the house, cased the place, then returned to kill her that night."

They were going to have to find Joe Beatty fast. Four women were dead. Was he responsible for all of them?

CHAPTER 27

From the stage, Ray Olson looked out at the crowd, which was bigger than usual, especially for a Monday-night concert. There were even quite a few people he didn't recognize as friends or family or regular concertgoers. Maybe this Summer in the Park concert series would broaden their audience. This was the second time this summer that they had the opportunity to play someplace other than Lincoln Prairie, which might help bring people into town for the fall and winter series. They were playing Tchaikovsky's Symphony No. 5 again, by popular demand, and even though he would admit that nobody played it quite like the Chicago Symphony Orchestra, he was always pleased to play with this orchestra because they were good. And tonight, his new trombone was exactly right. If only he had a sip of water. . . . They were all playing so well tonight. He hoped his slide wouldn't stick. Whether it was the warm night or the stars overhead or the attentiveness of the crowd, they were all really outdoing themselves.

After the concert, Ray stowed his horn and his wife's cello in the trunk of the car.

"Nice crowd tonight," he said as they headed home.

"You really hit those high G's in the fourth movement."

"That coda is my favorite part of the piece." He usually judged his performance on how many notes he wished he could take back. Tonight, there weren't that many.

"I love these summer concerts. And after a weeks' vacation, even playing on my first day back at work was okay."

They had gone to Minnesota, where he had grown up on a subsistence farm. No electricity until he was eight, no indoor plumbing, no telephone. His parents sold the farm while he was in high school. Now his mom grew tomatoes and he and his wife went to visit every summer for a week.

They lived east of Sherman Avenue in Lincoln Prairie. Tonight, there was little traffic. An old Chevy pulled in behind them, followed for a block, then turned at the top of the hill. The speed limit was forty-five, but from habit, Ray slowed as he reached a curve in the road. There was a traffic light just around the bend.

"They could have come up with a better place to put this light than a blind curve," he said, as he always did. Another block and a half and they would be home.

When the green light came into view, Ray speeded up. One car was slowing for the red light.

"Ray, is that the old car that was behind us?"

"I can't tell — he's got his brights on, the idiot."

He hadn't told her about that strange message on their machine from the police. Stay clear of the Beattys. Contact Detective MacAlister or Detective Jessenovik. He thought of it now.

As Ray entered the intersection, the other car accelerated, and he had to swerve to avoid hitting it. His wife screamed as they went into a ditch.

CHAPTER 28

When Marti arrived at the precinct Tuesday morning, Ray Olson was waiting to see her. He was a middle-aged, bespectacled man with a firm handshake, a friendly, open expression, and a warm smile. His left arm was bandaged and there were abrasions on his face.

"What happened to you?" Marti asked.

Olson explained.

"An older Chevy," she said. "What color?"

"Dark. I wasn't paying too much attention."

"Could you see who was inside?"

"My wife says it was a man. I was driving."

"I'll need to know your concert schedule for the rest of the summer."

Olson unfolded a piece of paper and handed it to her. "Any particular reason you think it might be the Beattys?"

"We're looking for them," Marti said. "Suspicion of murder."

"My God! Anyone I know?"

"I don't think so," Marti said. "You counseled the Beatty children while they were in foster care. How did you feel about them returning to their parents?"

"I advised very strongly against it. The judge ruled otherwise."

"Why didn't you think they should go home?" Marti asked.

Olson's expression was pensive. "I thought that eventually they would kill Natalie, or that if she lived long enough, she might kill herself."

Marti thought of Doreen Beatty.

"That kind of abuse doesn't stop," Olson said. "Joe was putting tape across Natalie's mouth and locking her in a trunk with airholes before she was two. He made her stand under a cold shower when she soiled herself. She didn't know what a warm bath was until she lived with the Muldoons. I wish Beatty would come after me," Olson said. "I don't think he's man enough."

"Do you think he tried to run you off the road last night?"

"Beatty's enough of a coward to try something like that." He thought for a moment. "And the car pulled onto Sherman three blocks from where we live. Are you familiar with that area? There aren't many houses on that street. Lots of trees. He could have read about the concert in the newspaper. The kids knew I'm a member of the orchestra. Now that I think about it, it's not that far-fetched."

Marti didn't think so, either. So far, the

victims had been women. Beatty wouldn't have been hesitant about physical confrontations with women. On the other hand, he might want to put something solid, like steel and metal, between himself and another man.

"Be careful," Marti said. "Very careful. I'll have extra men at the concerts and assign someone to follow you home. And we'll increase patrols where you live. You've got to remain on your guard, and report anything at all that seems the least bit suspicious."

After Olson left, Marti checked her in basket. "When they went through that pile of clothes in the McHenry house, they found some tools people use for doing ceramics."

"Compania Ortega," Vik said.

"That's my guess," Marti agreed.

There were more lab reports. "Here's something on Ortega. The blood samples and skin scrapings are not compatible with those of her fiancé." She was glad he was no longer a suspect. "The clay sample found at the Admunds place matches samples taken from the backyard in McHenry, but there was no match on the pollen — Rosinweed and black-eyed Susans."

"That narrows it considerably. Not much land left where wildflowers can grow, not with all of these subdivisions and condos they're putting up."

Marti read through the reports from the officers who canvassed with Hayes's composites of the Beattys. "Nobody at the Ship's Out recognized anyone."

"Drunks, that doesn't surprise me."

"None of Sophia Admunds's neighbors did, either. We got seven positive makes in Ortega's neighborhood; all but one of them fingered Joe."

"If everyone had neighbors like that, our gang and burglary units wouldn't have much to do."

"The odd vote was for Max." A sudden thought occurred to her. "Do you think the boys are still alive? The way they just dropped out like that . . . maybe he killed them, too."

"Possibly. Natalie wasn't around to abuse anymore. The fun must have gone out of picking on Doreen. What's a guy like that gonna do?"

"We're going to have to run these in the *News-Times* tomorrow." Marti looked at Doreen's composite again. There was little resemblance between their composite of the pert blonde aged to thirty-seven, still quite attractive, and the woman they saw at Elgin.

"Great, that'll flush out a few more crackpots. What do you want to bet we'll see our friends Alma and Darred again?"

Marti didn't answer. First chance she got, she was going back to see Alma.

CHAPTER 29

Mr. Muldoon called the precinct Wednesday afternoon. By three o'clock, Marti and Vik were at Mrs. Muldoon's bedside. Machines clicked and whirred and there was a faint odor of medicine and body wastes. The tubing from four IV bags and the leads for a heart monitor disappeared beneath the sheets. Mrs. Muldoon's head was bandaged. She had two black eyes, a broken jaw, and a swollen, bruised face.

"Do you know who did this?" Marti asked her. "Was it Joe Beatty?"

Mrs. Muldoon turned her head from side to side.

"It wasn't?" Was this just a random mugging? Marti thought. "Was it someone you knew?"

Mrs. Muldoon looked from Marti to her husband. She moaned as if she was trying to say something.

Mr. Muldoon patted her hand. "It's okay. We just thought it was Joe Beatty."

She nodded, then shook her head.

"Beatty?" Marti asked.

A nod.

"Joe?"

No.

Then who? Dear God, was one of the sons involved? They were just boys, teenagers. Damn. With reluctance, Marti said, "Vaughn?" He was the oldest.

Tears trailed down Mrs. Muldoon's face.

"Max?" Mr. Muldoon said.

Another moan, and a nod.

"He helped her put in a rock garden," Muldoon said. "They picked out everything and did all the work together."

Back in the waiting room, Mr. Muldoon paced for several minutes. The muscles in his massive shoulders tensed. He flung himself into a chair, legs sprawling. Marti guessed his shoe size at twelve.

"We've been foster parents for years," he said. "We've got two at home now."

"How long did you have the Beatty children?"

"Twelve and a half months. Not long enough."

"Why do you say that?" Marti asked. She wasn't sure she wanted to know. But if Max and not Joe was Mrs. Muldoon's assailant, she needed to know more about him.

"Nat and Max and Vaughn, they didn't trust anyone. They wouldn't let themselves like anyone. They wouldn't even acknowledge that they cared about one another. Those first few months were hell. Max and

Vaughn challenged every rule, every request, and they wouldn't allow either of us to touch them physically or emotionally. Nat was totally passive. She did everything that was asked of her, never objected, never dawdled, never talked back, never talked. By the time they were returned to their parents, Nat was finally beginning to trust us, and Max . . ." He shook his head. "He was just beginning to open up to me a little."

"And Vaughn?" Marti asked.

"He had settled down. He was so wired, so hyper when he came, that he bolted his food, didn't sleep more than six hours, couldn't concentrate in school. He was an honor student that last semester before they sent him back. I was really pleased that he managed to accomplish something he was proud of while he was with us. Vaughn really needed that boost."

"And Max?"

Watching as Mrs. Muldoon ID'd Max had been more than a surprise. Marti had thought of all of the Beatty children as victims. Maybe there was some mistake. They all looked so much like Joe Beatty that maybe, in the instant it took for her to recognize her attacker before being assaulted, Mrs. Muldoon had become confused.

"Max seemed to have some kind of center

within himself," Muldoon said. "Values maybe, or morals, or maybe just detachment. Sometimes being the middle child is an advantage. You know you're neither first nor last and you accept being different. I can't imagine what's happened to him. I'd never believe him capable of this."

"And Natalie?" Marti probed.

"Natalie was so eager to please, she'd break your heart." He sniffled, and Marti realized he was close to tears. "She just thrived on praise. She was starved for it. When she began to respond to affection . . ." He wiped his eyes. "She was so giving. I hoped that after a year, her parents would at least be willing to respond to that. We usually work with the courts and the social workers to get the children back with the parents. This is the only case where we actively fought to keep the children."

He walked about the small room, touching the walls as if he felt caged. "It didn't surprise me, not really, when Natalie disappeared. I wish to God I could believe her father didn't kill her. I wish I didn't know how many different ways he hurt her. Then I wouldn't have to wonder how she died."

Vik put his hand on Mr. Muldoon's shoulder. "It sounds like you did everything you could."

"Not quite," Muldoon said. "Max . . . will you let me know when you find him?"

"Sure," Vik said, and patted Muldoon's shoulder again.

"Hospitals," Vik said as they left. "I'd rather go to the morgue."

Within two hours of their return to the precinct, Lupe said, "Got it! Joe Allan Beatty died June twenty-seventh. His body is still at the morgue in Chicago."

"So much for Joe being our perp," Vik said. "I liked the idea of it being him. If Mrs. Muldoon is right, it must be Max. On the other hand, he and Vaughn look so much alike, she could be mistaken. How did Joe die?"

"Complications of cancer."

Vik gave a low whistle. "Occasionally, there is justice. A long, lingering death, I hope."

"He died at Cook County Hospital," Lupe said. "I don't think you'll get too much detail from them."

"June twenty-seventh," Marti said. "And that house was trashed two or three days later."

They had a problem getting the records released because they needed Vaughn Beatty's consent as next of kin. Marti put in a call to her former area headquarters in Chicago. An hour and a half later, the records were faxed in.

"Liver cancer, metastasis to lungs, stomach, pancreas, colon, bones — diagnosed in January, exploratory surgery, nothing removed, too advanced. He did not come in for chemo or radiation, was admitted in February, never left. There are half a dozen notations beginning in April where Joe requested that the feeding tube and IVs be stopped and he be allowed to die. Each time, Vaughn refused to allow it. They resuscitated in May and had to put Joe on a respirator. According to Vaughn, he became afraid of dying in his sleep and didn't want any more pain medication than was absolutely necessary. There are notations toward the end where Joe was refusing medication." Or Vaughn was refusing for him, since Joe was intubated and couldn't speak. "Cause of death was kidney failure and pneumonia. Sounds like his bodily systems were shutting down."

"Vaughn must have really been devoted to his father," Lupe said.

Marti found a notation indicating that Vaughn wanted Joe to have dialysis. "For whatever reason, he didn't seem to have been able to let go. That sure didn't do a damned thing for Joe but extend his suffering. It sounds like Vaughn not only wanted to keep him alive but alert as well; and with everything that was wrong with him, Joe must have been in one hell of a lot of pain."

Marti recalled what Ray Olsen said about Joe putting tape across Natalie's mouth before he locked her in a trunk. That wasn't much different from what Vaughn did to Joe. Maybe Vaughn was getting even. She read through the notes again. There was no mention of Max anywhere. Where was he while his father was dying? How did he feel about that? How much did those boys know about what happened to Natalie?

She shuddered as she thought of the trunk again, of that dark boxlike house . . . Alma Miller. She flipped through her notes, found Alma's fragmented dreams. A big empty house without windows — stars, animal sounds, the wind, the roar of the ocean. She read the notes again. House — Natalie; stars — Liddy Fields; animals sounds . . . maybe that was the Laws's cat purring. Wind . . . she couldn't think of anything — Sophia falling? It seemed far-fetched, but maybe. Ocean — Liddy again. Was Alma dreaming about this case? Did she know something else? Marti called Alma and got a recording. She left a message asking Alma to call.

"Marti," Lupe said. "Did you read this concert schedule?"

"Not yet."

"Well, there's a program tonight."

"Damn," Marti said. "I promised Ray Olson I'd have extra men there. I really don't think Max or Vaughn will go there, too many people. I do think whoever it is might wait in ambush somewhere. That seems to be his MO."

She called Ben. "Want to go to a concert tonight with the kids?"

Ben laughed. "This has to have something to do with work. Are we all going with you on a stakeout?"

"Sort of," she admitted, then explained.

Ben and the kids were at Prairie Park when she got there. She had contacted the lieutenant, explained her concern, and told him that based on the killer's MO, she did not expect him to go after Olson at the concert. On short notice, she managed to get eleven off-duty cops to show up, without promising them any action. The lieutenant added two squads to cover the area in case she needed backup. Lupe, Slim, and Cowboy agreed to a truce for the evening, and Cowboy even took off his hat to blend in better with the crowd.

The concert was held on the grounds of the Lincoln Prairie Historical Society, which was part of Prairie Park, and not far from a rambling white-frame Victorian that had been converted into a museum. Marti wasn't pleased with the location. There was too much land, too many trees, and the crowd was large and spread out. There were two buildings nearby, as well as the museum, a gazebo, and a small cottage. There were also several other small buildings in the vicinity. Not only that but also it was getting dark. It would become difficult to remain oriented if there was a pursuit. She felt too tired to chase anyone and wasn't looking forward to attempting it by moonlight.

Marti had distributed copies of the composites of Max and Vaughn, along with Olson's description. She and the other cops were in radio communication. She hoped they were also inconspicuous. Whether or not one of the Beattys showed up tonight, she had an obligation to protect Ray Olson. She confirmed Olson's location onstage — he played principal trombone. Then she walked to the trees along the perimeter of the crowd, where Ben and the kids were sitting.

She had identified three problems: Everyone was sitting down, which made any type of patrolling too conspicuous; she didn't have enough men to secure the perimeters; and the Beattys' composites had run in the *News-Times* today. She didn't know if Max or Vaughn was aware of that, or if anyone in the crowd would make the connection if they saw one of them. Theo and Mike knew she was working. They would stay close to Ben. They knew this wasn't the movies and that nobody would be shooting into the crowd.

The tree was on a slight rise, which gave her a better view. After the national anthem, she was glad everyone sat down. Isolating any movement had been impossible while the crowd was standing.

The evening's program featured show tunes, which were harder for Marti to screen out than classical, because she knew most of the lyrics. She had to force her concentration. She moved her chair to one side of the tree and found it easier to look around and look behind her inconspicuously.

The police radios were quiet until intermission. Lupe was to move to the steps of the portable stage and keep track of Mrs. Olson. Cowboy was on Mr. Olson and Slim was watching for Max Beatty. Lupe was wearing a bright red cap. As Marti watched, the musicians began walking toward the museum.

"The bathroom," Marti said. "I had the buildings checked out, but I didn't position anyone in there."

She gave two positions the okay to move closer to the museum. Intermission lasted fifteen minutes.

"Suspect sighted," Lupe said. "He's walking with Mr. Olson toward a rear door, east side of the building."

"Follow but keep back," Marti radioed. "We might have a hostage situation. Perimeter units two, three, seven, and eight, hold your positions. Everyone else move in. Stick to the plan. Do not approach the suspect. Keep the flashlights off unless I give the word."

She called for additional backup and, skirting the trees, headed for the east side of the museum.

Mr. Olson exited the building with a young male gripping his elbow. Olson was talking.

"They're heading in my direction," Vik said. "I can't tell which Beatty it is."

Marti circled until she was twenty feet from where Vik was standing, then watched as Beatty and Olson moved away from the light that came from the building and approached the shadows. She did not see a weapon. So far, Beatty had used whatever came to hand.

"Move in. Do not approach."

She signaled to Vik and raised her flashlight.

"Now."

In the moment that their flashlights blinded him, Lupe rushed in, knocked Beatty down, and grabbed Olson, shielding him. Beatty jumped up and took off, heading east. "Over here," Marti shouted, following with her gun drawn. She couldn't see him. Leafy branches hit her in the face. Dead wood snapped underfoot. She plunged ahead. Water splashed. Her feet were wet. Mud sucked at her shoes. Ahead, she could hear him.

"Here," she yelled to the others. "This way."

Mud gave way to tall reeds. Insects attacked. Her foot hit hard ground. She could hear him breathing. Behind her, someone cursed. Ahead, Beatty yelled. Marti pushed at the branches and ran faster. Suddenly, she saw the sky just ahead. Trying to stop, she slid and then tumbled a few feet down the side of the bluff, grabbing at the underbrush until she stopped. Crablike, she scrabbled down the side. Near the bottom, she reached him.

"Don't move."

He ran with a limp.

"Stop or I'll shoot."

He didn't.

"Halt," Vik yelled.

Turning, Marti saw Vik training his gun on him. She wanted him alive.

Marti sprinted after him, taking him down when she got close enough. Straddling his back, she took out her handcuffs and secured his hands behind him. Then she grabbed a handful of his hair and pulled his head up.

"Max?" she asked.

"Yes," he gasped. "Vaughn is killing them. Our pictures were in the paper. I came to warn Dr. Olson. I didn't know who else to tell."

Three hours later, in an interview room at the precinct, Marti was not convinced. Olson confirmed that Max had told him he was in danger, but that could have been a ruse. Vik took a turn with Max and then Marti tried again. Max looked underfed and exhausted. He smelled of dirt and old sweat and his hair felt oily when she'd grabbed it. He had to be living on the street. She wasn't ready to try being nice to him yet, but they had given him a can of diet pop, no sugar, no caffeine. There was no reason why he should be too alert.

"Where is Vaughn?" she asked again. They had twenty-four hours to charge or release him. She wanted closure on this.

"I don't know. I haven't seen him. I don't want to see him."

"Why not?"

He said nothing.

"When's the last time you saw your mother?"

He started to say something but changed his mind.

"Do you know where she is?"

He began picking at his sleeves. Marti got this reaction the last time she asked. This time, she decided to probe.

"Have you seen your mother since January?"

Max looked at her; his eyes were filled with questions. He slumped in the chair.

"Do you know where your mother is now?"

"Oh God, what has he done to her?"

Who? Did he know that his father was dead? Marti didn't ask.

"Is she dead? Is that why you keep asking me about her?"

"Is that important to you? Do you care?"

"Is she?"

"What do you think, Max?"

"I don't know. I didn't want to leave her. She wouldn't come with me."

"You left your mother?"

"I had to."

"How could you leave your mother, knowing what would happen to her?"

Max hung his head. "I couldn't help her. I couldn't do anything."

"But run, Max. You could run away and leave her."

"I couldn't stay there anymore." Tears streamed down his face, making streaks.

"But it was okay if your mother stayed. And now see what's happened."

"I didn't want him to kill her, too."

"Who else did he kill, Max?"

"Mrs. Admunds. And Miss Fields."

"Why did he kill them?"

"He hated them," he said, sobbing.

"How do you know it was Vaughn?"

Max trembled so violently that his whole body seemed to shake.

"He said he was going to kill them all."

"Why?"

"Because it was their fault."

"What was their fault?" Marti asked.

"Everything. Everything that happened to us when they found out about Natalie."

"Natalie is dead, isn't she?"

Max nodded, still trembling.

"Who killed her, Max?"

"I don't know."

"You do know, Max, and you'll feel better if you tell somebody."

"I was asleep. I don't know. Natalie just wasn't there the next day."

"I think you do know, Max," Marti said.

"No." He was crying uncontrollably. Marti didn't feel sorry for him. She waited until the crying subsided.

"If you want to talk to me, Max, maybe there is some way I can help you."

"Then tell me about my mother."

"She's in a hospital. Locked ward. She tried to kill herself."

"Again?" He was neither shocked nor surprised.

"Why did you think she was dead?"

"Because they beat her."

"They?"

"Vaughn and Dad."

"Did they beat you?"

"Vaughn did."

"Why?"

He shrugged. "Why not?"

"Who did you beat, Max?"

"Nobody."

"Have you ever wanted to beat somebody? Hurt somebody?"

He shook his head. "No. I just want . . . I don't know."

He wants a long shower, clean clothes, and some hot food, Marti thought with an unexpected rush of sympathy. At three in the morning, an egg salad sandwich on wheat from the machine in the basement, a bag of Fritos, and a cup of hot chocolate were the best she could do.

"So, what do you think?" Vik asked Marti when they returned to their office.

"I don't think Max is our perp." She had seen enough men who had killed more than once to know that the attitude wasn't there.

"Me, neither," Vik agreed. "And Vaughn is still out there. Back to square one."

"I think we can be reasonably certain that Vaughn was driving that old car seen near Ortega's house and by Ray Olson. So he does have some mobility. We also know that he's been someplace around rosinweed and black-eyed Susans."

"Nobody's spotted the vehicle."

Marti leaned against the wall and tried to keep her eyes open and talk at the same time. "Maybe Max will be more talkative after a few hours' sleep."

Vik agreed. "He sure didn't open up much when he was exhausted. Maybe we should go ahead and charge him so that we can have him transferred to the county jail and arrange for a shower and a jumpsuit. It's not easy spending an hour in the same room with him."

Marti yawned.

"Are you going to be able to make it home?"

She nodded.

CHAPTER 30

As Alma slept, she heard the wind again, a gentle wind, filled with the song of birds and the scampering of animal paws and pungent with the sweet smell of new clover and wild raspberries and tall grasses. This time she dreamed of a cabin with a wood frame and tan canvas top. The cabin was sheltered by boughs thick with leaves. Beyond the copse of trees, black-eyed Susans grew as far she could see. The sun was warm and the sky clear and Alma felt an immeasurable peace.

The light from the sun became bright enough to be blinding but felt warm and comforting. Hundreds of children's voices filled the air singing "Happy Birthday" in harmony. Alma could not ever remember feeling so much love.

"A good dream for a change?" Darred asked when Alma awakened.

"Ummm." She felt as if she had slept for hours and hours. It was the most comfortable and relaxing dream she had ever experienced. Maybe the dreams weren't all bad. Maybe others would be pleasant like this one. She told Darred about it.

"I think you dreamed about a cabin like that once before," he said. "Later, I'll look through the journal."

"I don't know if I want you to. Everything was so perfect. If I did have another dream about the same place and it was different then . . . if something bad happened . . . I want to remember this dream just the way it was."

When Marti woke up Thursday morning, the muscles in her legs and arms were sore as hell. She took a long, hot soak and some Tylenol and felt a little better. She was going to have to go jogging more often. Before leaving for work, she called Alma Miller but didn't get any answer. When she got to the precinct, there was a message from Vik that he would be late. Marti checked yesterday's *News-Times*. There was just the basic "have you seen" text under the Beattys' composites. What had really caused Max to seek out Olson? She sent out for a couple of Egg McMuffins and some orange juice and had Max brought in for questioning. Sometimes jail improved people's memories or made them anxious for fresh air, sunshine, and an unimpaired view of the hood. Marti didn't think this would hold true with Max, but it was worth a try.

Max eyed the food, then looked at Marti. His dark eyes were wary.

"I ate already," she said.

He wolfed the food down almost as quickly as his mother had. His face was clean, but because he hadn't been charged yet, he was wearing the same clothes and hadn't bathed. He seemed embarrassed, and he looked around as if he wanted to leave or at least sit farther away from her, but the interrogation rooms were just big enough for a table and two chairs. If he pushed the chair back, it would hit the wall.

"It's okay," Marti said. She had smelled worse. "Do you smoke?"

"No."

He had tested negative for drugs and alcohol.

"Why did you go to see Dr. Olson last night?"

"I saw our pictures in —"

"No, I don't buy that. What made you go there last night?"

"I went to the hospital last week to see how my old man was." He spoke without emotion. "They said he was dead."

"And?"

"When the old man got sick, Vaughn said he would kill them for what they had done."

"He loved your father that much?"

"Who? Vaughn?" He looked incredulous. "Vaughn hated him."

"You're losing me," Marti admitted.

"Vaughn hated all of us. The old man was sick for a long time. We thought he was just hungover. Vaughn, he became kind of the man of the house, you know? He um, he . . . With Nat gone, the old man didn't have anyone to pick on but Ma, and there wasn't much fun in that, not like there was with a little kid." He broke off, blinked rapidly, stared at the ceiling. "After Nat . . . everything just sort of fell apart."

Max took a deep breath. He wouldn't look at her.

"Vaughn, he um, he . . . Dad just picked on Nat. With Vaughn, it was everyone. First Ma, then me, then Dad. Vaughn would beat the hell out of the old man. That's why he was in the hospital when they found the cancer. He said he'd gotten in a fight, but it was Vaughn."

"Is that why your mother left?"

"I guess so. Ma and me, we knew to say nothing — we just let Vaughn hit us and get it over with. But the old man didn't understand. He always asked Vaughn why, or said he was his father, that he had never treated him like that. And Vaughn, well, he really got off on being begged and pleaded with. With Dad dying, it would have just been us. So we left. When you asked if I knew where she was, I thought Vaughn must have found her. I thought she was dead."

276

"Why did you go to Ray Olson?" Marti asked. She wanted to believe what Max was telling her, but Max and Vaughn had come from the same environment and he could be talking about himself.

"I read about Miss Ortega. Vaughn really hated her. Anyone who tried to be nice to him, he hated."

"And Ray Olson?"

"Dr. Olson made him cry once. I really liked Dr. Olson. He told me that I didn't have to be like my father, that I could decide not to be. It's hard sometimes, not to hit someone, not to drink, but I remember what Dr. Olson said. I don't want to be like my father. I didn't want Dr. Olson to get hurt."

"What about Mrs. Muldoon?" Marti asked. "Why did you go to see her?"

Max seemed puzzled by the question. "Mrs. Muldoon?" Then he put his hands to his face. "Oh God, I thought of her, but Mr. Muldoon is so big. . . . Vaughn didn't hurt her, too?"

"She says it was you," Marti told him.

He shook his head. "No. The only time I ever heard Nat laugh was while we were there."

Arms folded, Marti leaned back and looked at him. His head was bowed, his voice so low that she could barely hear him; he slouched in the chair. Someone who was very angry had attacked Mrs. Muldoon. Max wasn't angry now. Had he been angry a few nights ago? Or was Vaughn the one?

"Where is your brother?"

"I don't know."

"Max, what happened to Natalie?"

Max seemed to huddle inside himself. It was a curious kind of withdrawal, different from his mother's. He still knew where he was.

"Max, did you hurt Mrs. Muldoon?"

"No."

"Do you think Vaughn did?"

"Yes."

"Do you think Vaughn will hurt someone else?"

Max covered his ears with his hands. Marti didn't think it was a deliberate attempt to conceal information. It was more like the only way he had to run away. She leaned across the table, ignoring the odor.

"We have to talk with Vaughn, too. I need to find him right away. Think about it, Max. I'll be back to talk with you later."

Vik was sitting at his desk when Marti got back to the office. She filled him in. "He doesn't seem like a bad kid. I'd like to believe him. The trouble is, the whole family is so damned sick that it could be either of them. Maybe we should talk with Olson again. It sounds like he was able to make some emotional connections with the kids."

When Olson came in, Marti couldn't remember what last night's program had been. "I really enjoyed the concert last night — the first half, at least. My children did, too. Were you able to continue after your skirmish with Max?"

Olson seemed completely at ease. "Oh yes. It was a fun concert. And I must say, that young officer did a commendable job. As did the rest of you. How is Max? Where is he?"

"We're detaining him right now."

"How does he seem?"

"I'm sure he's been living on the street."

"That's a shame. He was doing so well with the Muldoons."

"And Vaughn?"

Olson shook his head. "No. Each child is different."

"Was Vaughn that much like his father?"

Olson leaned back and crossed his arms. "An astute observation. Neither was able to empathize."

"You opposed their return to their parents, Vaughn's return?"

He thought for a minute. "That placement was a wonderful thing and a terrible thing for those children." He was choosing his words. "It allowed them to experience something like a normal environment. Natalie thrived. When I told her she was going back to her parents, she never said anything. For the next three sessions, she practiced moving the play family in and out of the playhouse. And she talked to them. 'Don't be afraid.' 'Keep still.' And she sang 'Happy Birthday.' " He was silent for a moment, then gave her a wry smile. "Natalie never had a birthday party until she was with the Muldoons. At our last session, she brought in all of her toys and said good-bye to her dolls. She said her parents wouldn't let her keep them. I told her I would visit her just before school started, and if she wanted them, they would be in my car. I still have them." His smile became wistful. "You always hope that the parents have changed."

Marti looked at Natalie's picture. As soon as this case was over, everything would be filed away. Maybe someday she wouldn't remember what Olson had just said and get this lump in her throat.

"What about Max?" she asked.

"It was just as bad for the boys. For Max, it meant leaving Mr. Muldoon. Max was in a lot of pain. He hurt real bad inside. And he felt helpless. When we spoke alone, he didn't want to go back to his father. If he was with Vaughn, he couldn't wait to go home. Max was afraid, and in many ways bullied, and to a large extent, Max was a coward."

"The father is dead now." Marti told him about Joe Beatty's death but didn't mention anything that Max had told her. "How does this change things?"

"Vaughn needed an idol, someone to look up to. He picked the wrong person. His father could never tell him he measured up, or that he was good enough, or even that he could do something right. The one time he did something good, made the honor roll, and Mr. Muldoon and I let him know how proud we were, he cried uncontrollably. Vaughn was constantly striving to please someone who could not be pleased with anything. Vaughn functioned in anger."

When Marti explained the odd way Doreen and Max behaved, their way of somehow not being there, Olson said, "They aren't. Somehow, in their minds, when reality is too much to handle, mentally they go someplace else."

"Did Natalie do that?"

"Yes. A great deal of the time."

"Thank God for that," Marti said.

Marti tried to reach Alma again. There was still no answer. She felt too depressed to tell Vik about her conversation with Olson but then decided to, anyway. "My gut feeling, Vik, is that either Max or Vaughn could be our perp. They're like flip sides of the same coin. I hear what Muldoon and Olson say, and I agree that Max seems like a nice kid and Vaughn does not. But I've run across too many killers who looked and acted like choirboys to be taken in by Max."

"I know," Vik agreed. "I want to believe him, too, but you're right. If we just had enough evidence . . ."

While she finished writing her notes, Vik grumbled about the lunatic fringe and needles in haystacks. Then he took a turn with Max.

"I heard about the pizza you ordered in for him," Marti said when he came back.

"And I heard about the McMuffins. What the hell, Marti. Even if he did do it, everyone could use a little kindness, and I doubt that he's ever had his share." He got some coffee. "Too bad his tennis shoes didn't have enough tread to have any dirt wedged in the sole. The ones we found after Ortega was offed are the wrong size. I knew we were in trouble when they found that clay and the pollen. That might be the only break we get in this case."

"We've got to charge him or let him go before midnight."

"We've got time."

"Ten hours. Did he tell you anything?"

"Nothing I can use, but I think he wants to," Vik said. "I think he's real confused. Maybe Olson should see him. Would he?"

282

"I don't know. Olson said Max was a coward."

"Well, if he's telling the truth, he got brave enough to warn Olson."

Lupe came in.

"Read through all of the notes, Torres," Marti said. "Think like the perp. Where would you go? Where are you safe? What do you need to protect? Where are you comfortable? Where did you do something that you're proud of, something that's important? He went back to the house in McHenry for a reason. Safety, maybe. It's also where Natalie . . ." She didn't want to say *died.* She didn't know that yet. "Wherever he's hiding, that means something, too. If his father was buried, I'd have the grave site watched."

"There's always the morgue," Vik said.

"Good idea," Marti agreed. "Let's send a composite. Maybe Vaughn's been hanging around. Now that I think of it, it wouldn't surprise me at all if when we found Vaughn, we found Natalie, too."

Marti called Alma Miller again. Vik scowled as she spoke with her.

"Here you go again, MacAlister. She's a crackpot, a yo-yo who sees things."

"She has dreams."

"What's the difference? It's all in their heads. You just can't keep away from these types, can you? Next, you'll have her traipsing around looking for four-leaf clovers."

"Black-eyed Susans."

"You ever wonder why you gravitate to these loony types, MacAlister?"

Alma was pleased to see Marti. "I just made a fresh pot of coffee," she said. "We were in Wisconsin again."

Darred was in the living room, thumbing through a book. The room seemed even smaller with him there. Three suitcases took up most of the floor space. Marti suggested that they sit on the porch.

They sat on plastic molded chairs with a small matching table in between. The porch was shaded by large oaks that made the day seem cooler than it was.

"I know you've come about that woman Liddy Fields. And I haven't tried to block anything, but I haven't thought of anything else."

"Have you had any more dreams?"

"Nothing to do with water. And nothing real bad. Last night, I had a good dream."

The woman Marti had grown up around knew enough about their gifts to allow them to come. And because they were respected for their gifts, they were pleased to be helpful. For all that Alma would like to help, her reluctance must have driven away many dreams.

"Tell me what you dreamed about last

night." It might help if Alma thought about something positive, she thought.

"Oh, I was in this cabin in the woods, and I felt so calm, so happy. Everything was so perfect, so peaceful. And then . . ." She laughed. "My dreams are so crazy, even the good ones. I heard a whole choir of children singing 'Happy Birthday.' "

"What?" Marti said. Olson had said Natalie sang "Happy Birthday" in his office.

"That's what I said. 'Happy Birthday.' But you know, it was as if the song blended in. It didn't seem strange at all to hear all those children singing."

"Describe the cabin," Marti said.

"Well, there were trees, with flatland around them and kind of a hill on one side. The cabin was like a house at the bottom and a tent at the top. It was as if I had just woken up and I could hear the birds and see the sky and it was just a beautiful summer day. When I told Darred, he thought the cabin was something I've dreamed about before, but I'm sure I didn't, because I'd remember a dream that made me feel that good."

Something nagged at Marti. "You told me something about Darred and the dreams."

"Oh, the journal. He's looking through it now to see if he ever wrote anything down about a cabin or even just the woods."

They went inside and joined Darred on

the couch. The journal was a large cloth-covered ledger. The edges of the pages were worn, as if Darred had thumbed through them many times. Most of the entries were brief. They went back twenty years. Darred was working his way forward. Each entry was dated. Some had illustrations.

"What are the little red notations?" Marti asked.

"Oh, that means there was a newspaper article that I thought might be connected with the dream, something that happened at about the same time."

"Can I see those?"

"Sure."

He came back with a shoe box. Marti went through the clippings until she came to the same one about Natalie Beatty that Liddy Fields had cut out. She tried to speak calmly. "Why did you keep this?"

Alma looked at it. "I never dreamed anything about this, did I?"

"I believe so," Darred said. "Don't read it now and get yourself all upset." He turned to Marti. "I never show her any of these. She usually doesn't read the papers after the dreams. Just in case."

"Where is the journal entry about the dream?" Marti asked.

Darred flipped through the pages. "Here it is."

The date was the night Natalie disappeared. Alma took the journal and read the entry.

"That dream," she said. She closed her eyes and squeezed her hands in her lap. "That dream."

"You remember it?"

"I always remember if I read about them. That's why I don't. It comes back to me now as if it had just happened."

"What do you remember?"

"Dark," Alma said. "It's so dark. I can't move. I can't scream. I can't breathe. Keep still. Keep still. I'm so afraid." She buried her face in her hands and cried.

While Darred comforted her, Marti picked up the journal and looked at a sketch next to the entry.

"Is this the place?" Marti asked when Alma was calmer.

"Yes. As soon as I dreamed of that cabin, all the fear went away. Strange, isn't it? Now I've dreamed of it as a place where there is peace."

There was no way that Alma could know what Ray Olson had told the police. Marti blinked rapidly at the sketch, convinced that she was looking at the place where Natalie was buried.

Darred wouldn't let Marti take the journal, even for the day, but he did agree to accompany her to the library to make copies of the entry and the drawing.

Darred had drawn an odd-looking structure. The top was pointed like a tent and the bottom half had a wooden frame. There were at least a dozen large trees and several small ones, and a clearing.

"Okay, MacAlister, what's this? Did your loony friend draw it for you?" Marti showed the copy to Vik. "Not bad," he said. "At least it exists, or it used to."

"You know where this place is?"

"Sure, in McHenry. Right off Old Mill Pond Road. My brothers and I went camping there. There was more to it than this back then. I hate to disappoint you, but it's not there anymore. The land is being developed."

"Is this the development that's been in the news lately? The residents object to the size of the houses they want to build or something?"

"They don't want condos or a senior citizens' complex or lots smaller than half an acre. It's been on TV and everything. They got that state senator to speak out against it."

"And this has been going on for over a year now and it's still not resolved. If Natalie is buried here . . ."

"If Joe happened to see it . . ."

"Or more likely, Doreen," Marti said.

"Yes," Vik agreed. "She's just nuts, nothing wrong with her intelligence. Joe . . . well, he was a drunk."

"Can you still find this place?"

Vik put down the sketch. "MacAlister, a nutcase gave you this. No way will I go anywhere near there."

"Vik, Natalie could be there."

He looked at her. "You really believe this stuff, don't you?"

Marti nodded. "Not always, but this time, yes."

"Oh well." He sounded resigned. "My wife believes that these miraculous appearances are going on in some town in what was Yugoslavia. She's been saying some prayer or other that whoever is showing up there helps us find Natalie. She's been praying for oddball causes for years. Sometimes she gets lucky."

CHAPTER 31

I'm not going to be associated with anything that's connected with a psycho — excuse me, psychic," Vik said as soon as Marti pulled over to the side of the road. Half the area had been leveled, and new homes were going up.

"Here," Vik said as they approached an area where a bridge was being built to span the Fox River. She parked near some uncultivated farmland. She could see a broad stand of trees in the distance, then more farmland.

They walked along a narrow trail overgrown with brambles and thistles. Vik sneezed three times.

"Goldenrod," Marti said. "It's around here somewhere. You're allergic to it."

"I'd better be able to breathe tonight."

The sun was hot, and within minutes they were both sweating. When they reached the copse of trees, they could see that the land just beyond it sloped down. Vik stopped and pointed. "The campsite was spread out along there, along the base of the hill, fifteen of those tents. They each held six of us. There were five more near the top of the ridge."

"Where would the tent in the sketch have been?"

"I don't know. It's changed a lot since then. There were more trees."

She took out the copy and unfolded it. "Look, see the configuration of the trees? Think!"

"I don't remember anything like that."

"Well, we'll just have to look for it."

"If it's still here, MacAlister, which I doubt."

It took another ten minutes of fighting the underbrush to reach the base of the slope. Marti could see the meander of the Fox River.

"I've got stickers all over my slacks," Marti said.

"This was your idea," Vik reminded her.

He sneezed again. Marti stopped. The yellow flowers weren't goldenrod. They were rosinweed.

"Maybe we should go back," she said.

"Why? Giving up?"

"That's rosinweed, Vik. And I bet if we look around, we'll see black-eyed Susans."

"Not that again. It's been nothing but a distraction. If this case comes down to that . . ."

"Let's just walk back. Then we'll let someone who looks like they belong here wander through, okay?"

On their way out, they got the name of the developer. Within half an hour, he was there. This time, Marti waited while Vik and the contractor who was leveling the area went in. Marti could see the man's arms waving expansively, as if he was describing how everything would look one day soon.

"We didn't find the trees," Vik said. "At least I don't think so. But I ought to be able to drum up some old pictures of the place and we'll have another look-see."

"What's got you so fired up?"

"An old maroon Chevy with lots of rust."

Marti felt her heartbeat accelerate. "Where is it?"

"There's a bunch of pine trees at the far end of the base of the slope and an access road from the construction site. Hard to see it, the trees are so dense."

"Anyone inside?"

"I didn't get that close, not with one civilian and no backup, just radio contact."

They called the local force and the Sheriff's Department. The car was empty. Within an hour, the Chevy was staked out. Marti and Vik stayed inside a trailer on the construction site. The air conditioning felt good, but it was too far from the action.

When it got dark, they moved into position not far from the vehicle. Because sound carried too easily, there would be no radio communication unless it was a dire emergency. They were spaced out, in pairs, at twenty-foot intervals, depending on the topography. The sheriff's deputies hadn't wanted Marti this close — in case she had to go to the bathroom, they said. But in Chicago, they hadn't called her "Iron Bladder" for nothing. She nudged Vik. He frowned. They had to watch, listen, remain alert, and make a field decision about what to do if Vaughn approached.

An owl hooted, and Marti was sure there were bats nearby, too. She had seen bats at the zoo, but she didn't like them. She heard the rustling sounds and thought of rats, reminded herself that she wasn't in the city, then reasoned that rats would be out here, too. She glanced at Vik. They couldn't even whisper. He mouthed the word *raccoon,* but she didn't think he was certain.

They sat there for a long time before a loud snap got their attention. There were a few more cracks as a dark figure approached the car. Vik held out his flashlight. Marti nodded. They waited until the car door opened. Then they switched on the flashlights. Two dozen lights came on all at once and the car was surrounded. Vik hauled Vaughn Beatty out and patted him down. Marti cuffed him. The sheriff's deputies transported him to Lincoln Prairie.

"Piece of cake," the deputy told her while they were booking him. "He's already bragging. You won't have any trouble getting him to talk." Marti made sure Vaughn had been Mirandized. She called the state's attorney. She didn't want him to get off on a technicality.

CHAPTER 32

Marti and Vik went to the interrogation room, this time to talk with Vaughn. It was a few minutes past midnight. They had read through the statements from the deputies who had transported him. The young man had done quite a bit of talking, and he knew details — such as Liddy Fields's bathing suit tearing during her struggle — that few other than the killer would know. Vaughn had been Mirandized before he was transported, and as soon as he reached the precinct, he had signed a statement waiving his rights. Everything was in good order.

Vaughn stood when they came in. "Good morning, Detective." He extended his hand. Vik ignored it and motioned to him to sit down.

Vaughn gave Marti a look filled with contempt, then smiled at Vik. "How can I help you?"

Marti signaled Vik to do the talking and moved out of Vaughn's direct line of vision. Vaughn was an animated, energetic version of Max. He was an attractive young man with an earnestness that made him

295

seem both boyish and somehow mature. His hair was combed neatly, his shirt and jeans were clean, and he smelled of aftershave or cologne. He seemed eager to talk, but Vik said, "We can have a public defender in here in twenty minutes. This can wait."

"No!" For a moment, the pleasant demeanor slipped. "A lawyer?" He sneered. "Provided by the state? You expect me to trust one of those bastards?" Then the boyishness slipped into place. "I don't think we need an attorney, sir. All you want to know about is the murders."

Vik shifted. He was as uneasy with this eagerness to talk as Marti was. But she had seen this exhibitionist tendency more often than Vik, and frequently welcomed it. She was confident a confession would stand. She wasn't sure of how much supporting evidence they would have. The evidence tech was still going over the Chevy.

"What would you like to tell us?" Vik said.

"Should I just start at the beginning?"

"That seems like an appropriate place."

He described slipping into the water and gliding over to Liddy Fields and pulling her under.

"She was strong for an old lady, tried to fight back. If we hadn't been in the water, I would have hit her a few times to calm her down."

"Why did you do it?" Vik asked.

Vaughn ignored the question and launched into a description of Sophia Admunds. "She sure had gotten old since the last time I saw her."

"When was that?"

"When I was a kid and I watched her sitting on the steps crying because I pulled up all of her damned flowers, rosebushes, everything. I destroyed her yard."

"Why did you do that?"

Vaughn laughed. "She followed me all over that house without remembering who I was," he said. "She never shut up. Bad plumbing, bad wiring, flooding in the basement. She sure didn't want nobody buying it." His expression changed. "Complaining, complaining, complaining. I could hardly wait to push her down the stairs."

"Did you know she was selling the house when you went there?" Vik asked.

"No. I was going to ask if someone I went to school with lived there, pretend I was lost and ask to use the bathroom. I just wanted to see what the place looked like and maybe leave a door unlocked. She started in about not wanting me to appraise the place, so I appraised it."

"Why did you want to push her down the stairs?"

Again Vaughn ignored the question and proceeded to talk about Compania Ortega.

297

He spoke with pride of waiting for her in the garage.

"I made sure she saw me first, just for a split second. You should have seen her face. And then" — he brought his hand down on the table — "man, I timed it just right. She didn't have time to make hardly a sound."

There was no mention of Tyrell Laws.

Vik looked at Marti with an expression close to disgust. She gave him a small nod.

"What about Miss Laws?" Marti said.

"What about that bitch?"

"Why don't you tell me?"

"Oh? What is this? Your butch cop routine?" He turned to Vik. "Did you give her permission to speak?"

Vik's jaws got rigid but he didn't answer.

"What about her?" Marti persisted.

"She was a nosy-assed bitch," Vaughn said, "just like the others. Just like you! We no sooner get back home again and she comes snooping. Her fault, all of it. Well, I fixed her! And guess what? When I get out of here, your ass is next." He jabbed his finger at her. "I don't allow no bitches to fuck with me. You understand that?"

Marti smiled at him and said nothing. She knew just how to yank his chain. And she understood why he had killed. She walked out of the room and watched through the two-way mirror.

Vik pulled his chair a little closer. "So, Laws came to your house?"

"Yes, sir. You know how nosy women can be."

Vik nodded. "When you lived in McHenry?"

"Yes. She had the nerve to find out where we lived and come asking about Natalie."

"I can understand why you wouldn't appreciate that."

"If they had left us alone, none of it would have happened. We'd still be living in Lincoln Prairie; the old man would still be alive. He would still have his job. It would just be the four of us, if hadn't been for them."

"What about Natalie?"

"She was nothing but trouble."

"How so?" Vik asked, lowering his voice.

"Do you have any sisters, sir?"

"No. My mother died when I was a kid. It was just me and my dad and my brothers."

"Did your dad beat her?"

"Who? My mother? No, he didn't."

"Then I bet she didn't complain all the time, or else you lucked out and she died before she became a real nag. With us, it was my mother's fault that he lost his job, her fault that he drank. And every time he went out the door, she was telling us what a bastard he was."

Vik was jiggling his foot. He wanted to get out of there.

"I heard about your dad, heard how you were there for him."

"He really suffered at the end. He was all swollen and he hurt so bad, he just couldn't keep still. And that tube down his throat — every time he tried to say something, it jerked. His throat must have been raw. I sat with him the whole time. He just lay there moaning. It was awful."

"Too bad he got pneumonia."

"I know. He would have lasted a few months longer if he could have got put on dialysis."

Vik hunched forward. "We're going to look for Natalie in the morning, Vaughn."

"You won't find her."

"You wanna bet? We know where she is." He pulled out a copy of Darred's sketch, unfolded it, and spread it on the table.

Vaughn looked at him, surprised. That was his only reaction until he laughed.

"The old man said they were going to dig there, put up some houses. He said you'd find where I put her. I beat his ass for saying that. He didn't say it no more."

Vik stopped jiggling his leg. "Look, Vaughn, I don't know just what we can do about all of this, but you are cooperating. I will let them know that. Now, Natalie has been missing a long time. There are a lot of people out there wondering what happened to her, a lot of people who are going to think you're a pretty rotten human being when they find out. Maybe, if they knew your side of it, they'd realize what kind of person you really are."

Vaughn's demeanor became almost shy. "We were starting over again. The house wasn't as nice, but things were almost like they used to be. The Muldoons never understood Natalie. She tricked them into thinking she wasn't bad. They didn't know how sneaky she was. When we went back home, she started stealing food. She thought she belonged in a bed. She had to be beaten before she would get into the tub. And Dad, he said that if he did it, at first anyway, and they found out, we'd have to leave again. So I had to help him, just for a while, just until Natalie was trained again. She was bad when we left her in the basement. She sneaked upstairs for food until we caught her; then she tried to get out the window. I had to bring her up to my room and tie her up and put tape over her mouth so she'd keep still. When that Laws bitch came to the house and said she was going to call them again, I knew Natalie couldn't be trusted to keep her mouth shut; so when I brought her upstairs and tied her up, I put tape over her nose, too. Not that it did any good. The old man still lost his job. We still had to move again."

Vik looked exhausted when he came out of the interrogation room. "My God," he said. "My God." He rushed down the corridor to the men's room with his hand over his mouth.

CHAPTER 33

At nine o'clock Friday morning, Marti and Vik were back at the site of the old camp. The developer who owned the land had a team ready to dig. An assistant coroner was there to identify human remains. Marti and Vik tackled the bramble and thistle and dense underbrush again. This time they were both wearing hiking boots and jeans.

"Damn," Vik said as mosquitoes and gnats swarmed in small clouds and attacked. "I think the insect repellent attracts them. Maybe we should have worn cologne."

Except for their hands, they were exposed only from the neck up. By the time they were halfway up the tree-shaded slope, Marti was convinced the bugs were biting through their clothes. The soreness from Wednesday night's roll down the bluff was gone, but the muscles in her calves were aching. She would go jogging with the kids tonight.

At the top of the slope, they came to a clearing that went halfway around the perimeter. Segments of an old trail were bordered by clusters of black-eyed Susans. Marti checked her sketch. It was unlikely that any trees had been cut down. When she found a configuration that looked like Darred's drawing, she stopped.

"Here," she said.

The dirt was packed down and difficult to break. They dug with spades and picks. Marti and Vik stood in the sun and swatted at insects and sweated as the team of twelve men made slow progress. It was several hours before one of them found a slender bone about six inches long.

"Lower arm," the assistant coroner confirmed. They excavated the remains of a small child. Some of the bones were missing. Marti and Vik watched until everything that was still there had been found. After the assistant wrapped the bones in a small bundle, they followed him down the slope and watched as he stowed his parcel in the trunk of his car. Neither Marti nor Vik said much as they drove back to Lincoln Prairie.

When Marti got back to the office, the evidence tech who was working on the old Chevy called to say he was having a field day. He wasn't sure which samples would match what, but there was plenty of evidence in the vehicle. Vaughn was just as eager to sign a statement confessing to the homicides as he had been to tell everyone about them. They had him on videotape as well. Vik had become so upset listening to Vaughn that Marti didn't discuss any of this or say anything when the Sheriff's Department called to let her know that Vaughn had been transferred to the county jail.

The jail was new, and there was direct supervision. The guards mingled with the inmates, who had quite a few privileges if they behaved. Structure, consistency, routine, discipline, and safety seemed to come as a relief to some of them, not to mention having a bed, toilet, and shower facilities and eating three times a day. Sometimes she wondered what would happen if children were provided with all of those things from birth. Today, she thought about Vaughn. She wondered how quickly he would learn to be respectful to the female deputies. Too bad they couldn't give him cold showers when he wasn't. Eventually, he would reach a prison that had a "hole." Then if he didn't behave, he would come to understand the meaning of being locked in a closet and subsisting on bread and water. At least he wouldn't have to eat dog food.

Max was being held as a material witness and awaiting transfer to a juvenile facility. Mr. Muldoon had received permission to see him and was hoping eventually to take him home. Marti put in a call to Denise

Stevens. "The Muldoons are among our most successful foster parents," Denise said. "Losing Natalie was devastating for them. Now that Max has made it to the juvenile system, I'll do what I can."

Max hadn't believed her when she told him Vaughn was in jail. She showed him the story in the newspaper, but he couldn't read all of the words. "I was afraid," he said when she told him Natalie had been found. "I was always so afraid. I didn't do anything to help her."

The physical differences between Max and his brother were so subtle that until Marti talked with them, she didn't wonder why people couldn't tell them apart. Marti thought their personalities were different, that perhaps Max was a survivor. At least she hoped so.

The lieutenant came to Marti and Vik's office. He didn't look as if he had gotten much sleep lately, either.

"You did an amazing job," he said. "And, Torres, that includes you."

Lupe beamed. "Thank you, sir."

"Incredible, isn't it?" the lieutenant said. "He's only eighteen. And as insane as all of this is, the state's attorney expects him to be found legally sane."

"It's scary," Vik said.

"Well, at least Natalie has been found."

Dirkowitz walked to the window and stood in the sunlight. "I don't think any of us expected a different outcome. At least this gives it closure." He turned. "You two must be exhausted. Finish up whatever you can't postpone and then go home. The rest of it will keep until tomorrow. This has been one hell of a forty-eight hours."

Marti picked up the picture of Natalie. She tried to think about children singing as she put it into an envelope, put the envelope into the Beatty folder, and put the folder away.

Marti was alone in the office when the uniform knocked on the door.

"This was left at the desk for you, ma'am." He handed her a canvas sports bag. A piece of paper stuffed in the side pocket had her name printed on it.

"Who left it?"

"This girl came in and kind of stood near the door with it. It's Friday night, ma'am, pretty busy downstairs. I might not have remembered her if it wasn't for the black eye. I assumed she came in to take out a complaint. I looked up and she was gone, but not the bag. We checked it out pronto. Nothing in there but clothes and personal effects."

Marti looked inside. Old clothes — jeans, T-shirts, and a clean but wrinkled dress shirt and a pair of slacks. Deodorant, a toothbrush, and toothpaste. A tool like the ceramic knives recovered at the McHenry house. Marti's heart beat faster. A ring with what looked like a real gem in an antique setting. She thought of Liddy Fields. A gold chain, broken, but with the clasp intact, as if it had been deliberately broken or snatched from someone's neck. Tyrell Laws? A silver napkin holder. Sophia Admunds? A stained and dirty business envelope. She removed the contents. A death certificate for Joe Allan Beatty, Vaughn's Social Security card. Something folded and unfolded so many times, the creases were worn — a grade-school certificate of merit, Vaughn Allan Beatty, Honor Roll.

When Vik came in, she said, "Christmas might have come early this year. A young lady who wishes to remain anonymous brought this." She gestured toward the contents of the sports bag. "It seems that Vaughn liked to take trophies."

CHAPTER 34

Gilbert Admunds called the precinct Monday morning. The Sunday papers had run front-page stories about Natalie. It had been on the national news. Sophia Admunds, Liddy Fields, Compania Ortega, and Tyrell Laws had all figured prominently. One newscaster described them as heroic.

"We talked about all of this last night," Gilbert said. "I guess we all just got so wrapped up in our own lives, and then there was Mother, and we had no idea of what was going on with her. We didn't have time. In any case, we've decided to set up a memorial for her with a local child-abuse agency. If there's anything else we can do, let me know."

As Marti hung up, she thought of Gilbert's unruly children; then she remembered what Vik had said about the younger brother outshining the oldest one. It seemed as though Gilbert wanted to continue to outshine Warren, even though his mother wasn't there to acknowledge it. Maybe he did remember Sophia singing lullabies in Polish.

A few hours later, a young woman was shown to Marti's office.

"Yes," Marti said.

"I'm Coralana Jones. I called yesterday . . . about the picture in the newspaper."

Lupe had taken two calls. Marti consulted Lupe's notes.

"Liddy Fields." Maybe Fields did have a daughter. Short and plump, with her hair in dozens of braids, Jones didn't look anything like Fields. She had very smooth dark skin.

"I was referred to the coroner's office. I just came from there. The woman I spoke with said that you had been very persistent in finding out who . . . hurt her . . . and in trying to locate a relative. I guess there was something on the news Sunday night, but I missed it."

"I'm very sorry about the circumstances, Miss Jones, but I'm so glad there is someone."

"I'm not her daughter," Jones said. "I'm a friend, kind of. Liddy worked at a school where I lived — a juvenile center. When I got out, we kept in touch. I'm in college now, getting my master's in education. I don't have any money to bury her, but Liddy had no family. I had to come at least."

"No family? She never mentioned a child?"

"She said she had a baby once. She said it died. Spinal meningitis. She said she couldn't save her. There's nobody. Just me. And I can't even —"

"Let me make a few phone calls," Marti said.

Marti called Whittaker's Funeral Home. The director was Denise Steven's brother-in-law. He agreed to handle the arrangements.

Next, she called Gilbert and asked if his family would be willing to defray the cost of shipping Liddy's body to Tennessee. "She was alone most of her life," Marti said. "It would be nice if she could finally be near someone who cared about her." Gilbert agreed.

Natalie's funeral was held the following Saturday. Dozens of floral arrangements surrounded a pink casket. An eight-by-ten photograph of a smiling Natalie was on a table surrounded by the toys and dolls she had given to Ray Olson. The church was filled to capacity. Max was allowed to sit with Mr. Muldoon. Marti stood beside Ben. Theo, Mike, Joanna, Sharon, and Lisa were there, too. Vik came with his wife. A rabbi spoke, then a priest, then Reverend Douglas.

"We have come here today — family, friends, clergy, government officials, police officers, social workers, teachers, strangers, and friends — because it takes a village to raise a child and today this village — Lincoln Prairie, Illinois — has lost a child. We come together today to mourn the loss of that child and celebrate her homecoming in heaven."

EPILOGUE

When Marti got up the next morning, she filled a carafe with decaf coffee, spooned raspberry fruit spread on two pieces of toast, and went out to the deck. It was hot already, but the deck was sheltered on either side by tall oaks and the table had an umbrella. A rabbit sat in the grass near Theo's garden, its brown and white ears alert. Marti thought about chasing it away, but if it ate squash, it would be more of a friend to her than a pest. She wasn't looking forward to a winter filled with tureens of squash soup. She had decided to reduce her fat and caffeine intake, but only until her annual physical the following week.

The noise surprised her. Insects hummed. Sparrows squabbled in the evergreens, cardinals chirrupped, and it wasn't even seven o'clock. The children would be getting up for Sunday School soon.

She had gone to Joanna's game yesterday afternoon and to a concert in the park with Ben and the boys last night. In the week since they had found Natalie, she had even found the time to pick up Ben's ring at the jeweler's, although she hadn't given it to him yet. She had gotten to bed by midnight every night this week, but she was out of the habit of getting eight hours' sleep at one time and woke up after five or six hours still feeling tired. Joanna and Theo were pleased that she was jogging again, even though she went to the indoor track at the "Y." Maybe this week she would go to the Forest Preserve. Maybe not.

There was a sudden scrambling sound as a family of squirrels scampered down a tree trunk, jumped on the deck, and ran across the railing. Marti tasted her coffee, which had cooled, drank it, and then poured another cup. She reminded herself that there would be no caffeine pickup today. She ate cold toast, drank more coffee, and watched as a mourning dove flew in and out of a yew tree, bringing breakfast to its mate. They had all been disappointed, especially Theo, when last year's eggs weren't fertile. This year, both eggs had hatched. Theo said the birds were good parents.

Ben came out on the deck just as the squirrels were making another foray across the railing.

"You're up early again," he said. "Still not sleeping well?"

"I've just got to get back into the habit," Marti said.

314

"I think you're a little depressed about the Beatty case."

Instead of disagreeing, Marti took the box with his ring out of her pocket. "Happy birthday," she said, then burst into tears.

Ben gave her his handkerchief. "Pretty bad, huh?"

"Yeah." Marti sniffled and blew her nose. "Pretty bad." She got up and walked to the railing.

"Feeling better?" Ben asked after a few minutes.

"I suppose. I don't usually react this way. I've seen more dead children than I can count. This is just sleep deprivation. I'm overtired."

"I've noticed that," Ben said.

"No, really, I, um . . ." She wouldn't be falling apart like this with Johnny. Johnny had understood that she was strong. What would she be doing if he were here? Storing up stress for a coronary?

"Come on," Ben said, "sit down. You look worn out."

She sat at the opposite end of the table.

"Tough cop," he said.

"You've got that right."

He moved closer. "Big Mac. Five ten, a hundred and sixty pounds, carries a Beretta, don't take nothing from nobody. I bet nobody messes with you, either."

"If they did, I'd be their worst nightmare."

Ben chuckled. "Now I know a strong, sassy, independent woman like yourself don't need no man looking out for her or anything like that, but do you suppose that every once in a while I can sneak up on you like this?" He kissed her neck. "Or this?"

She turned toward him.

"Damnedest thing," he said. "I got me a whole lot of woman here, one who don't need no looking after, and all I want to do is take care of her." He handed her the box with the ring. "Open it."

Instead of the signet ring she had picked out for him, there was a diamond solitaire inside.

"This isn't —"

"I know." He held up his hand and showed her his own ring. "I bought that one for you," he said. "If you'll wear it."

Marti smiled. "As long as you remember — strong, sassy, independent, and Beretta!" She held out her hand and let him slip the ring on her finger.

DATE DUE
